COMMODORE HENRY GALLANT

H. Peter Alesso

THE HENRY GALLANT SAGA

Midshipman Henry Gallant in Space © 2013
Lieutenant Henry Gallant © 2014
Henry Gallant and the *Warrior* © 2015
Commander Henry Gallant © 2016
Captain Henry Gallant © 2019
Commodore Henry Gallant © 2020
Henry Gallant and the Great Ship © 2020

Other Novels by H. Peter Alesso

Captain Hawkins © 2016
Dark Genius © 2017
Youngblood © 2018

COMMODORE HENRY GALLANT

H. Peter Alesso

hpeteralesso.com

© 2020 H. Peter Alesso

This is a work of fiction. All characters, dialog, and events portrayed in this book are fictional, and any resemblance to real people or incidents is purely coincidental.

All rights reserved.

No part of this publication may be reproduced, stored in a retrieval system, or transmitted, in any form or by any means without prior permission in writing from:

VSL Publications

Pleasanton, CA 94566

videosoftwarelab.com

Edition 1.00

ISBN-13: 9781704389165

∞

It's the detours a warrior takes

that make his struggle remarkable.

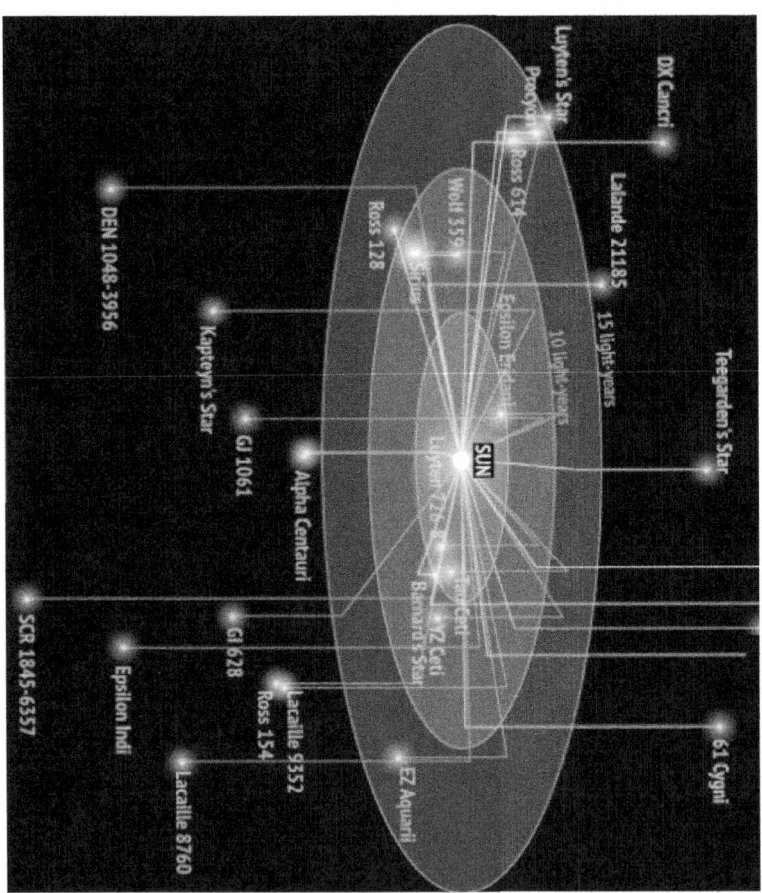

Stars Surrounding the Solar System

United Planets—Task Force 34

Captain Henry Gallant

    2 Spacecraft Carriers – *Constellation, Courageous*

    Starfighter Space Wing

        72 Viper I

        96 Viper II

        12 Hawkeye

    2 Battlecruisers – *Indefatigable, Indomitable,*

    12 Cruisers

    48 Destroyers

    2 Stealth Recon – *Warrior, Invidia*

    12 Auxiliary Support Ships

Marines

Major James Steward

    1st Marine Raider Battalion

Chameleon

    The Great Ship

Titan—Home Fleet

Admiral Zzey

    6 Spacecraft Carriers – *Vampiri*,

        Starfighter Space Wing

            216 Fighters

            216 Bombers

24 Search
6 Dreadnought
6 Battlecruisers
96 Cruisers
288 Destroyers
288 Auxiliary Support Ships

Titan Gliese-Beta Planetary Defenses
24 Orbiting Battle Stations
120 Ground Missile Bases
444 Fighters

Asteroid Fighter Base
Fighter Command & Control Center
216 Fighters
24 Search

CONTENTS

Chapter 1 Unidentified Flying Object

Chapter 2 The Matryoshka Doll

Chapter 3 The Great Ship

Chapter 4 Portrait

Chapter 5 Persuasion

Chapter 6 Treasure Map

Chapter 7 Liberty

Chapter 8 Constellation

Chapter 9 Everyone Lies

Chapter 10 President-Elect

Chapter 11 Hell Week

Chapter 12 Lord Protector

Chapter 13 Lucky 7

Chapter 14 Treaty

Chapter 15 Diary

Chapter 16 Secrets

Chapter 17 Cruel Business

Chapter 18 Operation Damocles

Chapter 19 Trojan Horse

Chapter 20 Hawkeye

Chapter 21 Gotcha

Chapter 22 Launch

Chapter 23 Renege

Chapter 24 Gung Ho

Chapter 25 What If

Chapter 26 Thunder and Lightning

Chapter 27 Over the Top

Chapter 28 Decoy

Chapter 29 Missile Lock

Chapter 30 Raining Fire

Chapter 31 Engage

Chapter 32 Tethered

Chapter 33 Better Late

Chapter 34 Homeport

Chapter 35 Home

From the Author

CHAPTER 1

Unidentified Flying Object

Lieutenant Rob Ryan was bored. He hated the mundane tasks of being a squadron leader. He liked 'fast'—the faster, the better. But that wasn't happening today as he cruised over Earth in his Viper.

He was stuck with the tedious job of training his new wingman, Glenn Holman, in strafing maneuvers against the Antarctic target range.

As he executed a simple wingover in his starfighter, he was about to comment on the poor performance of his novice companion when out of nowhere, the world changed, shifting with shocking suddenness.

That's not possible!

He instinctively flung an arm across his face to ward off the seemingly endless wall of steel that had materialized in front of him.

I must be hallucinating!

Heart-throbbing fear gripped him.

But there is something *delicious* about fear. It starts with bitter panic and grows into sour excitement—until, at last, comes sweet courage.

Ryan pulled his arm down, tightened his grip on the thruster, and yelled, "Hard to port! Max thrust! Flip gyros!"

Over the next several seconds, he concentrated on avoiding a collision with the mountain of metal.

In the first second, he felt the chest-crushing weight of 14 g's as his Viper began the pivot.

In the next second, he fought down the blackness of his vision, narrowing into a tunnel as 20 g's tested the limitations of his pressure suit.

By the third second, he felt as if he was being squashed like a ripe tomato—right before he blacked out.

Several seconds later, he came to, blinking against the glare of the sun. Even as he aimed his ship toward it, he heard Holman gasp, "I can't ... make it ..."

Almost immediately, Ryan saw the brilliant red-white explosion of Holman's Viper as it went splat against the steel wall.

He sighed with relief when he saw an escape pod spiral toward Earth.

The July blizzard howled across the high plateau of the Amundsen–Scott South Pole Antarctic Station, leaving a record snowfall of crystalline ice in its wake, and blustering so hard that the Earth defense sensor arrays were blanketed under the full fury of the whiteout. So powerful was the blizzard that sharp flecks of ice pierced the multilayered protective gear of the technician sent to investigate some minor static interference. As the man crawled toward the besieged sensors, his hands lost feeling despite the well-insulated flex-gloves. A large scavenger Skuas bird dive-bombed him, causing him to grab hold of the lifeline tether to keep from falling off the sheer rock cliff.

"Damn!"

"What's wrong?"

Against the howling of the wind, he could barely hear the question. During the six-month southern hemisphere 'night,' the wind blew at 160 km/h, and the temperature dropped to minus 89 °C. Despite the harsh conditions, the dry atmosphere and extended darkness made the station the Earth's best location for astronomical observations. It had every conceivable type of sensor from microwave telescopes to neutrino detectors. The sensors were so accurate and dependable that the people of Earth rested reassured of their absolute safety.

The man gripped the taut cable as he spoke into the mic, "Why do I always get the crap jobs?"

"Just do it. And better hurry. Something big is brewing."

Inside the station's geodesic dome, a sensor operator

screamed, "Contact! Contact over Melbourne. It's massive!"

The duty officer came over to the operator's station. "What's the problem?"

The operator pointed, his finger trembling in shock at the image that filled his screen.

Flabbergasted, the duty officer asked, "Where did that come from? No unidentified contacts have been reported!"

"It just popped up out of nowhere."

"That's impossible."

"I'm telling you. Everything was normal, nothing but standard traffic patterns, and then WHAM! There it was."

"Have you run a diagnostic on your equipment?"

"Look at the other sensors. They all show the same thing. We have a man outside checking some minor glitches, but nothing that would explain this."

"It isn't a colossal malfunction? Do you think this is a bona fide contact?"

"Yes, sir!"

In the stunned silence, the senior chief operator said, "Designate contact as Tango 101, in geosynchronous orbit over Melbourne."

Still unable to grasp the situation, the duty officer asked again, "Why didn't you spot this earlier?"

"I'm telling you; it wasn't there before. It came out of nowhere. As if it dropped out of cloak."

The dark eyes of the duty officer met the senior chief's

gaze. "That's impossible. Even in a blizzard, our active sensors can penetrate any cloaking device within a million kilometers of Earth."

As he shook his head, the chief's white hair fell across his grizzled face, but his eyes stayed steady. "Until now."

The officer asked, "What type of craft is it?"

"Nothing in our databases even comes close. Visual images are starting to come in now. Man, it's the strangest thing I've ever seen."

The officer's eyes bugged out. "Oh, my Gawd! That's incredible. It's enormous. What the hell is it?"

His hand smacked the red alert button, and his voice echoed over the base-wide intercom. "Activate planet defenses. Scramble standby fighters."

A second later, he said into the emergency radio, "Put me through to Admiral Devens, immediately."

When Admiral Devens responded, the duty officer said, "We have an unidentified flying object over the capital."

"Notify all missile and laser batteries to target the contact, but hold fire until further notice," said the admiral, unruffled. "Have fighter command scramble all fighters and intercept the UFO."

"Fighter command, this is Lieutenant Ryan flying *Constellation's* Viper 607. I have Tango 101 in sight."

Like a minnow swimming next to a blue whale, Ryan flew alongside the alien craft examining its features.

He said, "Tango 101 is a monster ship that looks like a giant squid. It has an ellipsoid body thirty kilometers in diameter with protruding spikes seventy kilometers long. This Great Ship is beyond the combined resources of all the planets."

"Is it broadcasting?" asked the command center.

"Negative, according to my sensors. It has not responded to radio communications, and I can detect no emissions at all, hostile or otherwise."

"Shadow it, but do not engage."

Twelve hours later, President Kent addressed the nation. "My fellow citizens, what you have heard is true. We have detected an alien vessel over Earth, but there is no immediate cause for alarm. Planetary defenses are on full alert. Our space fleet and fighters have surrounded the unknown spaceship. We do not know who these beings are, but they are not our Titan enemy. And though victory against that enemy may still seem a long way off, we are prepared to face any challenge they set against us. This new arrival has so far taken no hostile action, and our hope is that they will prove to be a benefactor rather than an adversary.

"So, we must be patient until our visitor decides to speak. Until then, I am certain that you will all remain as brave and resolute as our proud space navy that stands guard protecting us at this moment."

Over the next several hours, news stations maintained uninterrupted coverage around the world. Opinions were divided over accepting the president's optimism. Some listened to the vitriolic counterargument made by presidential candidate Gerome Neumann. He advised swift and total annihilation of the aliens who had violated Earth's space.

When it seemed that the tension couldn't get any greater, an astounding event occurred. A shuttlecraft departed the Great Ship and landed at the Melbourne spaceport.

The Great Ship

CHAPTER 2

The Matryoshka Doll

Henry Gallant frowned as he entered the Solar Intelligence Agency. It held some of his most unpleasant memories. The facility reserved one underground location for its ultra-secret investigations where conspiracy, mystery, and suspicion were layered like a security protocol onion.

A guard scanned his comm pin and led him to a small side conference room. As he settled into an uncomfortable steel chair, a familiar voice said, "Hello, Henry."

He looked up to see Julie Anne McCall walk into the room and take the seat across from him. Immaculate as always, she had an impressive presence. Although only a captain, her accomplishments had already made her a legendary figure. Her name was known throughout the fleet and within the highest levels of political circles. She lived in the center of a web of intrigue and secrecy.

Even after knowing her for years, Julie Ann remained an enigma to Gallant. At times she had rescued him from certain disaster—only to turn around and send him into a ruinous adventure.

He wondered which side she would show today.

"Why did it take so long to grant me access?" demanded Gallant. He was seething with frustration after being excluded from one of the most significant events in his lifetime. The SIA had clamped down on the media and kept the most basic information hidden—even from the military.

"Do you deny the widespread military implications of this event?" he asked as an image of his ship flashed into his mind.

"Of course not," said McCall pursing her lips.

"My ship needs to know," he said, pressing his hands against the top of the table. "*I need* to know what's happening."

She avoided his eyes. "High-profile events take some finesse."

Her grin only served to irritate him further. Bristling at her nonchalant manner, he demanded, "Tell me about that ship."

"Don't be so impatient. We'll get to that in good time." She sat up straight, her spine never touching the back of her chair. She opened her tablet, scrolling through the screens while Gallant tapped his fingers.

As he watched her, he realized she was surreptitiously watching him. She was like a doctor examining a patient to search out all his innermost secrets.

She's testing my reaction.

He crossed his arms.

When the information she sought was displayed, she became intent and pressed her lips tight.

She said, "The Chameleon have initiated a dialog. It turns out that that name is particularly appropriate. They are not only great at building stealth ships, but their bodies are stealthy as well."

Gallant brought his brows together.

Her face was pale and earnest as she spoke. "The Chameleons can alter their appearance by stimulating changes in the spaces between chemical crystals in their skin. The process shifts the wavelength of reflected light to alter their skin color and texture. It's natural, built-in camouflage, sophisticated enough that they can transform before your eyes."

"Such a natural talent must have motivated their interest in stealth technology," suggested Gallant.

"And if their ship is any indication, they're great at it."

"You've spoken with them?"

"A low-level delegate landed in a shuttle at Melbourne. I was fortunate enough to be one of those who interrogated him. He was not very forthcoming, and we learned little."

Gallant heard the strain in her voice, something he had never heard before.

She's upset. Worried, even.

Although McCall's face was pale, her words were quick and sharp. "He greeted us warmly but was guarded about their technology and the current status of their war against the Titans. Their ambassador has so far refused to meet with us. We're also having trouble with their language. We can catch all their words but somehow never quite grasp the meaning. It's as if we can't listen fast enough to capture their full intent."

"You can't understand them?"

"Oh, they speak perfect English."

"What then?"

"I can't believe a single word they say."

"Why not?"

"They are playing a multilayered game of intrigue beyond anything I've ever encountered. Even while we were in discussion with their representative, they attempted to access the SIA AI system. Fortunately, our firewall alerted us. We weren't able to block penetration, but we could track it."

"You're sure it was them?"

She sighed. "I'd better start with what we do know. Their Great Ship, as intelligence is calling it, has such incredible stealth that they penetrated every one of our planetary defenses without detection."

"I've seen those reports. Quite a feat."

"It was. After all," she grimaced, "the ship is a hundred kilometers long,"

"Are they cooperating?"

"Not so much. After the first few days of their visit, we uncovered some disturbing information."

"Which was...?"

"From our earlier collection of alien artifacts, we already knew the Chameleons have an AI chip implanted in their brain. Their representative was open about their special abilities. That's why we sent for you. We're hoping, with your AI talent, that you might be better at understanding their meaning."

Gallant kept his expression neutral, though an electric thrill ran up his spine.

"They speak with a normal voice, but we've become convinced that they use their AI chip to communicate telepathically among themselves. The AI chip also gives them access to encyclopedic knowledge—data updates, background information, who knows what else. By using a neural interface, we were able to pick up on a little of their communication process." She gave a grim smile. "They didn't tell us this, of course. Meticulous surveillance has its benefits."

Gallant considered the enormity of such a discovery.

"What do you want me to learn from them?" he asked.

She turned her tablet toward him, pointing to a file marked Top Secret: ULTRA. At first glance, he noted several unusual symbols.

"We want you to join a delegation to visit the Great Ship and meet with the Chameleon ambassador. We need to know why they're here, what their capabilities are, what they want from us."

"And?"

"Whatever else you can find out. We've learned nothing about their society from our interrogations so far," said McCall with a shrug. "Discover as much as you can. Admiral Collingsworth concurs with my recommendation that you join the ambassador's delegation. Your designation will be as a linguistic interface."

"An interface? Nothing more specific?"

For the first time, McCall's face relaxed a bit. "It's vague to give you leeway. Admiral Collingsworth is particularly interested in finding out more about their stealth technology. The president suggested opening discussions about a treaty, or even a trade agreement. Our goal would be to set up an alliance. Above all, we don't want them as our enemies."

Gallant's mind sparked from idea to idea on how he might approach the aliens. "Even if they refuse to assist us, the information they have about the Titans and the surrounding star systems could be invaluable."

McCall closed her tablet with a click and looked at Gallant, her eyebrows raised. "Any more questions?"

"How soon can I visit the Great Ship and meet their ambassador?"

McCall stood up and crooked her finger. "Follow me."

CHAPTER 3

The Great Ship

Gallant was surprised to be welcomed aboard the Great Ship by a Chameleon woman who was a head taller than him.

She said, "Prepare to adjust your mind to a new scale of reality. The scope of what you are about to experience is beyond your imagination. This Great Ship houses over one million inhabitants and can travel between the stars at warp speed in stealth mode."

Her words were prophetic. Gallant and Ambassador Charles Salinger's delegation entered a world of contrasts—it was as if they stepped into Jonathan Swift's 'Land of Brobdingnag.'

The compartments were enormous, with ceilings rising a hundred meters over their heads. Even more astounding were the corridors. They were multilane highways full of motorcars scurrying in all directions at reckless speeds.

Gallant was amazed that crumpled vehicles weren't piled up at every junction. He could only assume that they were controlled by AI. People in jetpacks darted overhead like swarms of bees. But the true enormity of the ship was brought home when the woman herded them into a car and drove through tunnel after tunnel until they lost all sense of direction. Her path took them through compartment after compartment. Some were crammed full of electromechanical equipment. Others were living quarters or shopping areas. They flew so quickly that none of the delegation had time to take in all they saw, much less ask any questions.

Sitting beside Gallant, McCall said, "The more I see, the more questions I have." She remained quiet throughout the tour, but she wore a pin-sized video recorder on her lapel and spoke detailed notes into it. The rest of the delegation spoke amongst themselves.

When they stopped at an intersection, she threw a ball in the opposite direction that they were traveling in.

"Why did you throw that ball?" Gallant asked.

"That was an SIA spy drone, and I sent it to fly over areas of the ship that the guide doesn't intend to show us. I told you these people are not forthcoming."

"Is the guide like the envoy you spoke with?"

"Yes."

Gallant asked, "How are we going to negotiate?"

25

"These people are very different than the methane Titans, but they are still alien to us. I've seen some subtle signs that give me concern."

"What signs?"

"There are many mysteries here. I've detected lies and deception."

He reminded her, "You just released a spy drone."

"In self-defense."

"Aren't you afraid you might sour things if you're caught?"

"I'm more concerned that things might not be what they seem. We can't blindly trust them. Our people want peace and security. That's hard to provide in the middle of a war. It would be impossible if we faced an even greater threat, and we weren't prepared. We must learn about these strangers to prevent being surprised by something very bad. That comes at a price. We must verify their words and actions."

Finally, the guide stopped their vehicle in an expansive atrium and said cheerfully, "The ship's central levels including administration offices, living quarters and amenities. The lower levels are for engineering and cargo. Finally, the upper levels are for ship control and weapons."

The guide said, "This central area will give you a more intimate look at our city-ship. This complex supports a luxurious lifestyle for our Chameleon inhabitants, upwards of a million people. You see how we value beauty and artistry as well as personal expression."

She showed them the central part of the spaceship, which was a bustling city of a million people. It had an elaborate complex that supported a luxurious lifestyle for the Chameleon inhabitants.

She said, "The architectural design is more of a boutique hotel with many thousands of rooms than a ship. It has the intimate ambiance of a private home despite many communal living spaces. All the amenities are scaled, from a choice of chic and elegant, sleek and contemporary, to quaint and homey. There is an artistic décor. Some of the apartments are closed within the hull, while others offer viewports. There are shops and restaurants for meal service designed for a variety. Many entertainment options are available, including shows and movies. The stores reflect people's heritage through color and art. Many inhabitants prefer an outdoor style complete with trees and greens."

McCall turned to Gallant and asked, "A city with civilians on board? Why would they do that? Is it good to have their family aboard? Are they keeping them safe or putting them in harm's way?"

Gallant said, "I can imagine two reasons; they're needed to maintain the full service of the ship while keeping their family safe. They are always with you but always in danger. Personally, I wouldn't like that."

"How many does it take to fly and fight this ship?"

"One this size? I've no idea," said Gallant.

"The technology must be well advanced over ours."

"Not necessarily. They built big, but that doesn't prove they are advanced in more than a few technologies."

"How does it make you feel?" she asked.

"Envious. Frightened. Hopeful."

"Hopeful?"

"Hopeful that they might become a friend."

During their hair-raising journey, the guide kept up a lively chatter about her people. Gallant learned about the Chameleon, but the content was superficial and missing essential details. She steered clear of discussing the military aspects of the ship and concentrated on describing the homes.

The Great Ship was like a giant squid. It was a bulbous ellipsoid sphere thirty kilometers in diameter with its narrow backside showing the massive ship's propulsion engines. Projecting from the narrow forward edge of the swollen vessel were seventy-kilometer-long laser spines. Gallant guessed that the spines were nuclear-pumped super-lasers capable of creating great energy. A weapon of such enormous explosive power was one he wouldn't want to experience.

"Look at the super-laser beams." Salinger asked Gallant, "Can you guess about the firepower of this ship?"

"I would imagine one blast could sink a continent or worse."

Gallant examined indications of stealth and laser capabilities. He walked past the intelligent paneled walls without concentrating on any of the notices that appeared for his benefit.

The Chameleon woman stopped and let them stroll across a walkway, smack-dab in the middle of a well-manicured garden park. It even had a water fountain and statues.

When Gallant entered the park, his reaction was unlike what might be expected from a ship's captain. He was enthralled in the joy of the people. He had a sense of excitement as he strode along the intersecting causeways. Everyone who passed nodded a warm greeting. What was most curious was the posture of the people—shoulders back, head high—proud, almost haughty.

Soon the Chameleon woman indicated the tour was over, and they returned to the car. She whisked the delegation to the ambassador's suite. As expected, the ambassador lived in the most prestigious luxury suite in the deepest depths of the Great Ship under guard by a strong security service.

A colossal door swung open, admitting Gallant and the delegation, to a cavernous reception room. They were wide-eyed at the elaborate decorations and artifacts exhibited. Guards and civilians were standing along the sides of the chamber.

As Gallant walked along a carpeted path toward a raised chair, he considered the woman seated there. At first glance, she appeared quite old but handsome. As he watched, her appearance transformed into a dazzling young dark-skinned woman. Then for a fleeting moment, he seemed to see Alaina.

No. As he approached, he saw the Chameleon woman was

distinctly old, though she possessed a sense of regal majesty. Her appearance gave the impression of an exotic mixture of human races. A series of ridges gave her face a curious pattern, and her skin shifted from a smooth alabaster-white through a rich range of subtle colors. Both the texture and the color seemed to reflect her mood. Even her robes shimmered with every movement—a fascinating distraction.

"Welcome visitors from Earth. We greet you with peace and friendship. Please make yourselves comfortable we wish to become acquainted."

Salinger said, "Thank you, Madam Ambassador. We extend greetings from our president and our people. We hope that our two peoples will become fast friends."

"I have every expectation that that will be the case," she said and focused her gaze on Gallant.

As if reading his mind, she said, "I assure you, I am quite ordinary."

Gallant was certain that was not true.

She let her hand slide over his face, which might have been an affectionate jester.

She sighed, and the corners of her mouth turned up. "But my name is not so very ordinary. You may call me Aurora."

Touching his cheek again, she said, "I'll stay and talk to this stranger for a while."

Her melodious speech sounded more like a song than a statement. And a strange thing happened to Gallant when she touched him. He felt she knew him—as if all his flaws and imperfections were exposed. Her awareness of his inner thoughts seemed so intimate that he blushed and drew back.

He imagined she said, "You are a gifted one, and so you are impatient for change. But you are young, and that's your flaw."

There was no sign that anyone else heard these words.

She put another thought in his mind. "Look at me. I was once like you. Now I am old, but I am happy. Be calm, and over time you will find your way."

Her next words were spoken aloud for all to hear. "In times long past, my people flourished on several nearby star systems. We were happy and successful people until the coming of the Titan two centuries ago."

The eloquent elocution of her golden voice was hypnotic and captivating.

"Since then, we have endured perpetual warfare. Several of our stars systems have been obliterated, including the Ross system, which you now occupy. The Titan may believe we are already allied as a result of your last action there."

Gallant felt a great wave of sadness overtake him as if Aurora were broadcasting her emotions at him. It sent a shiver down his spine.

Aurora said, "Our Lord Protector has wisely sent me to Earth to learn from you what you fear and what you love. You should not fear that we will use the opportunity to harm you."

"That is reassuring," interjected Salinger, who moved in

front of Gallant.

Aurora faced the Earth ambassador. "Dear friend, there can be no escape from the endless political intrigues of living. People will scheme to survive, one and all. We will live and die on our ability to understand and control the passions of survival. It is timeless, but you will find no evasion from me."

"Your failure will also be our failure as well," said Salinger.

"I agree."

"We wish to find a way to convince you of what we offer for mutual benefit."

Ambassador Charles Salinger tried to direct the discussion to more specific objectives. Gallant listened and said little. Unhurried, Aurora conversed about politics as if it were an abstract concept.

As she talked, Gallant didn't focus on her words. Instead, remembering his role as an analyst, he tried to absorb the emotional tenor behind her words and said little in return. Specific characteristics of the alien's behavior puzzled him. He couldn't explain her actions without considering subterfuge.

He was curious about her intimate reaction to him and wondered if she were trying to hide her real intentions. Clearly, she had her own agenda, but she did not appear to be uncomfortable with his ideas. That his mind seemed so transparent to her made him narrow his eyes, but the revelation did not make him think he had mistaken the situation.

She is not an immediate threat to Earth.

Gallant said, "You said we had seen your military might, but all we have seen is this one Great Ship. Will you give us more information about your strength?"

Aurora did not show any displeasure. She nodded and gave him a smile. "We built ships of ordinary size for commerce and transportation. But rather than fleets, we build massive individual warships that dominate our enemies. This Great Ship is a planet killer, our ultimate weapon—a nuclear-pumped super-laser capable of concentrating enough energy to cause a planet-wide extinction with one shot."

She sighed as if regretting where her story led. "Construction of such behemoths required time and resources. We could only build one Great Ship for each star. The ships had a perfect stealth technology that rendered them undetectable. But the cloak required so much power that they couldn't fire their weapons or accelerate unless they dropped the cloak. It took time to power up its shields and weapons, which made them vulnerable.

"When the Titans first attacked one of our stars, its Great Ship annihilated them. But they learned. When they returned, they didn't try to attack the Great Ship directly. Instead, they went after the planets. The Great Ship could not respond quickly enough to the smaller isolated skirmishes, and in the lulls between firing, the Titans attacked with overwhelming numbers and suicidal collisions. Some Great Ships were destroyed, and their star systems plundered."

She did not reveal how many Great Ships remained or how

many stars systems the Chameleon occupied. She sighed, "A balance of power now exists between the Titans and us."

Aurora shifted in her chair. "Long ago, I discovered the secret to power and success. I discerned the patterns that offer advantage or disadvantage, and how to take gain from each."

Gallant wanted to summon the words to persuade her to help in the war, but before he could form the reasons to make this powerful person help the United Planets, Aurora appeared to already understand.

She turned to Salinger and said, "You see our military might, and though our war with the Titans has reached a ceasefire, we may consider assisting you."

"I am gratified. What do you ask in return for your help?" asked Salinger.

"You have vast amounts of minerals and manpower. We could make good use of them. I propose that you permit us to establish an embassy here to learn more about you. You are invited to set up an embassy in our Cygni star system and begin negotiating a treaty. Once you meet the Lord Protector, he may grant you limited cooperation in your war with the Titans."

"Thank you, Ambassador Aurora."

The ancient woman stood up and said, "Since negotiations may take some time, I have a gift for you as a gesture of goodwill."

A guard brought in a large container containing computer components.

"This AI quantum computer will double your current

stealth technology."

As she walked away, Gallant thought,

Thank you.

CHAPTER 4

Portrait

A laina stood in the courtyard, focused on her painting. The bright southern hemisphere sun glinted on the medals that decorated her subject's uniform and accentuated his athletic build. The skirt of her flowered dress danced around her knees in the light breeze, making it hard for Gallant to hold still. She squinted at the canvas and dabbed with a fine-point paintbrush, delicately applying the paint to get just the right curve to his ear. With each stroke, she admired her subject but couldn't help frowning at her failure to fully capture his grace and rugged charm.

After a minute, she sighed and swabbed her broad brush in the white pigment at the center of the palette. Her frown deepening, she swiped it over the ear. The overcoat masked the flawed detail, and she leaned in to try repainting the errant ear for the third time.

When she first asked him to sit for a portrait, he had reacted with dismay.

"A photo would do just as well," he protested, thinking of all the demands on his time.

"Don't be absurd. A photo is nothing but pixels. A painting expresses your character. It's an emotional connection between subject and artist that brings your inner self to the canvas," she said and touched his cheek. "Besides, it's an expression of my love for you."

As always, she won him over. There was no escape, but there were benefits. Sitting for her gave him unlimited license to admire her stately beauty as she stood poised at the easel. He loved watching her expression shift as her paintbrush moved across the canvas.

"Alaina?"

She jumped; her concentration broken. "Huh?"

"You look so intense. Are we almost done for the day?"

"Hardly. I just can't seem to get the right shape on your ear."

"I'm sorry. I shouldn't have startled you," said Gallant. "I was just thinking about . . ." His eyes traveled over her body.

Flustered, she turned back to her painting, though her cheeks flushed pink.

He smiled, remembering the lesson when she offered to teach him to paint. He was already a fine sketch artist, but when she posed nude for him, very little paint went on the canvas.

When he reminded her of that exchange, Alaina's color deepened. She laughed, "It's the adventurous detours you take that make your life journey remarkable."

But just as quickly, she returned to her canvas and cast an appraising eye at Gallant's uniform and posture just as he fidgeted.

"Husband, I love you more than anything in the world, but if you move again, I'll kill you."

Gallant took a deep breath and tried to direct his mind elsewhere while maintaining his pose. He recalled his early days in the Navy when he was considered different and unwanted. Without genetic engineering, he was summarily labeled as inferior, someone to be ignored. Early on, he was shunned and ignored. While the indifference was a cruelty all its own, at least it was a passive exile. Over time, he learned to disregard the apathy of his contemporaries. Still, even after his years of achievement, many in the service still considered him a freak—an annoying disturbance to the proper order of things.

Instead of damaging his character, he drew strength from those who defied the common opinion and dared to befriend him. Their support nurtured his spirit; their selfless acts became his guide on how to treat others with tolerance and respect. They had helped him become a caring and kind person—one who could find and hold a wife such as Alaina.

I have the perfect marriage.

He was utterly devoted to Alaina. He loved everything

about her, even the small irritations that exasperated him. She had succeeded in wrapping him around her finger, which he found endearing rather than annoying. Though aware of her feminine tactics when she wanted something, he didn't mind indulging her because he recognized the sacrifices that she made for him.

They brought out the best in each other.

Inexplicably, his thoughts of Alaina were interrupted by an image of Kelsey that flashed into his mind. It was like stepping backward in time. An abstract reminiscence of an unobtainable long-lost chance that was now much regretted. He knew thinking about her was wrong, and he would never end up with her, but still, she lingered serenely in his thoughts—the one who had left him heartbroken years ago. Working with her on the *Constellation* had reignited dormant passions that he fought to suppress. Even now, with Alaina right in front of him—desirable, seemingly the love of his life—he had to keep himself from asking whether he was truly meant to be with her.

He blinked and focused his gaze on Alaina. "You're amazing," he said, and after her look of surprise, he continued, "I don't know where that came from, other than I am completely in love with you."

"I love you too," she said in a distracted voice.

After a final dab, she set her brush on her easel and put a cloth over the painting.

"Done?" he asked, moving close to touch her shoulder.

"For now." She sighed and stretched. "We should be getting home."

He gathered her canvas, paints, and easel while she wiped down her brushes.

Back at their small apartment, he stood the painting against the wall next to a small table that displayed her sculptures. The late-afternoon sunlight streamed in, highlighting her artwork.

Gallant looked around the room. Portraits, landscapes, and abstracts showed the range of her talent. Moving to the corner, he examined his latest sketch with a critical eye, observing all its complex flaws, as well as his effort to capture Alaina's true underlying beauty.

Alaina said, "I want to talk to you about my getting a job. I've completed my journalism degree, and I've been offered an internship with the Melbourne Herald."

For a second, he thought about the extra money a job could bring in. It would be heaven-sent to help reduce the mountain of debt they had accumulated in legal fees from his past court-martial.

"That's wonderful. Congratulations. The money will come in handy."

"Yeah, I know. There's just one small requirement I need to fulfill."

"What's that?"

"I have to submit a sample article . . . and I gave the impression that I could land an interview with someone who has firsthand knowledge of the Chameleons."

"Me?" he asked with raised eyebrows.

"Oh, no. I wouldn't put you in such an embarrassing position," she said. "I thought you might ask Captain McCall if she could spare a moment."

Gallant squirmed inwardly. He imagined the two women chatting about any number of awkward subjects—mostly his shortcomings.

What could go wrong there?

CHAPTER 5

Persuasion

Seeing President Kent gave Gallant a shock. The man sat propped up in his chair, powerful and vibrant as always from the waist up. The open-collar shirt and an old green sweater gave the illusion of peaceful relaxation. But his baggy trousers couldn't hide the slack legs so characteristic of his degenerative muscle disease.

The Secret Service agents stood closer than usual, like anxious nursemaids.

Gallant had heard the rumors, of course, but still, he hadn't expected the President's condition to be so advanced.

"Hello there, Henry. It's good to see you. Come in, have a seat," said Kent, his voice weary. "I've had my afternoon snack already, but would you like some refreshments? It's no trouble."

"No, thank you, Mr. President."

"Well then, perhaps you will indulge me a few minutes while I practice my music," said the elderly man. Gallant could hear the trace of wistful regret in his voice at the unattained dreams of Kent's youth.

Kent pushed a lever on his chair, which floated smoothly across the room to his piano, his security agents hovering behind. He spent a minute swiping at the music screen, pausing with a smile at Claude Debussy's "Arabesque."

Gallant let his mind wander with the delicate notes that filled the room. As the last note lingered poetically and faded into silence, he applauded with true delight.

"That was touching, Mr. President."

"Thank you. Thank you," he said. "I'm never shy about appreciating praise. I try to steal a few minutes to play every day. Otherwise, you know, the skill atrophies."

Kent grabbed the arm of one of the agents and lifted himself out of his chair.

Gallant stood up, surprised.

Another agent handed him a cane, and Kent lurched and hobbled toward the cabinet holding his family memorabilia.

"My doctors want me to replace my crippled leg with a prosthesis."

He stared at a photo of himself standing on a beach with his children, one of them sitting triumphantly on his shoulders. "Water is my natural environment. I love to swim and sail. Though if I were young now, I might choose space as my natural habitat.

Like you."

Gallant nodded. He could imagine the President as a spaceship commander.

"Sit down. Sit, Henry." The President waved at a chair. "Will you join me in a drink. I'm allowed one a day, and I'm going to need it now."

"Whatever you're having, Mr. President."

"You must be a tonic because I'm beginning to feel better by the minute," chuckled Kent. "But, I guess, I have to get down to business."

He paused and stretched his aching legs.

"If we only had some way to break the stalemate . . . I reached out to you, Henry, because ultimately, this war will come down to the ingenuity of just a few individuals."

The President looked suddenly careworn. "The people don't want to fight this war. It's that simple. Yet how do you *not* fight an enemy who keeps coming back for more?"

He shrugged. "What more can I do that I am not already doing? My political opponent is the most notorious liar of all time. I can't stand to hear his calumny. But that's the price you pay to be in politics. Neumann has been climbing in the polls, thanks to the Titan raids."

Teddy patted his shoulder.

"Please, look at this, young man," said Kent as he handed a document to Gallant that was headed "President—Eyes Only—Top Secret, copy: one of one."

As Gallant perused the document, Kent said, "I've received a copy of a report on how the Titans are treating our prisoners of war. Not good. We have very few Titan captives because of their suicidal policy. But we treat them humanely. They are fed and sheltered and given their methane requirements without torture or beatings. We have broadcast our treatment and asked for reciprocal behavior, but the Titans remain mute on this, as they do on everything else. We've discussed this with the Chameleon. They almost cried when they described their losses and treatment at the hands of the Titans."

He showed Gallant additional notes from a debriefing from the SIA and intelligence analysis from the fleet. Nothing in the document was a surprise to Gallant other than the lack of insight derived by the intelligence organization.

It was for this chat that Kent had summoned Gallant, for some intuition into the aliens and the war from a first-class mind. Gallant had no illusion that he held a secure place in the President's esteem. One wrong step and his opinion would be vanquished with all the other advisers who had come and gone over the years. But so far, he had been pretty prescient.

"The situation is now very grave," said Kent, sitting down. "And it is growing alarming in every dimension. There is concern about Elysium at Tau Ceti. The mutual defense treaty with our outpost planets was to be designed to share the burden of defense, but they don't all seem to shoulder their share. It was well understood that training and cooperation were necessary to act in concert. But it takes time to establish joint expertise."

Gallant said, "Their failure at Ross offset the Titan's early successes. The Titan had a sound attack plan based on solid doctrine. Their plan required complicated timing coordination between assaults and movements to different stars. But losing Ross was a setback for them. We need to press that advantage by disrupting their time schedule, which should throw a wrench into their entire strategy." He paused and took a deep breath, looking straight at Kent. "My idea is to carry the war directly to the Titan home star system, starting with a raid to Gliese-Beta."

"I've been talking to my advisers about your suggestion. The consensus is that it's extremely risky. Foolhardy even."

During their discussion, Gallant observed that the President was a gifted empath and a great listener. He would lean in, make eye contact, and nod reassuringly. His questions were always framed in a way to make clear he understood the premise. But now, Gallant saw something different, something new, a different posture to Kent's body, a tension in his shoulders. His earnest expression became slightly unbalanced as the corners of his mouth turned down.

"I just don't know," said Kent shaking his head. Doubt crept into his eyes. It was tiny, involuntary, and vanished almost instantly.

Gallant said, "A daring strike hitting the Titans' home world would be the most effective way to upset the status quo in the war."

Teddy said, "Such a blow will galvanize the public. They will rejoice at the news. I don't blame you for being cautious, Mr. President, but I believe in Captain Gallant."

Kent looked like he had received a shot in the arm. "Yes. Yes, let's do it."

CHAPTER 6

Treasure Map

The glass-walled headquarters auditorium was a tiered amphitheater with many seats. In front, a table was flanked by a dozen chairs. A whiteboard hugged one side and a flat-panel screen clung to the opposite wall. The room was rapidly filling up.

Gallant had often faced skeptical military and political audiences. But today the faces around the conference table—some of them familiar, some hostile—were especially grim and anxious.

His hands lay clenched in his lap. He didn't play with the cuffs of his uniform sleeves or tap his fingers on the arm of the chair, or even twitch an eyebrow. But under the table, his toes tapped an arrhythmic beat, counting off the seconds as the speaker prattled.

Normally, he wouldn't be so restless with someone giving a presentation of such importance, but today he was impatient. He had been anxious over planning and preparations for weeks. He'd listened to complaints and nay-sayers for hours. His head was buzzing with the whine of their disagreeable voices. The longer the discussion went on, the more unbearable the pressure became.

At least he kept his self-control long enough to avoid drawing frowns from around the room.

He sat as rigid as the guard at the door.

Lucky Marine. He wasn't wearing four gold bars on his uniform sleeve. He didn't have to sign off on the entire operation and face the consequences if it failed.

"During the six months since the Third Fleet relieved the Marines on Charlie in the Ross system, the Navy has fought six bitter and bloody skirmishes with the Titans in four neighboring star systems," said McCall. "Three were fought at close range, ship-to-ship, with gunfire the primary weapon. These actions were significant from a tactical point of view, although they did not result in a change of control on any of those planets."

Admiral Collingsworth added, "We haven't had a carrier engagement since Ross. But our fighter production has outfitted many new squadrons that are ready for action."

McCall said, "The Ross action was unique in several respects. It was primarily a carrier-to-carrier action but did include some direct ship-to-ship combat. It employed the latest innovations in stealth, point defense, and weapon batteries."

Gallant said, "We learned a lot from that action, including coordination of integrated space and land action."

An officer from Admiral Graves' staff, a pale chap with red hair, said, "I don't think that the Titans were seriously disturbed by their defeat at Ross. They would see it as a temporary setback."

Another officer said, "They will continue with their ribbon of frontline defenses. They're relying on their home fleet and a strike force sent to attack our systems."

"Knowing the enemy's intentions is helpful, maybe even admirable, but that doesn't mean we can stop them from carrying out their plans," said the staff officer.

Collingsworth said, "Nothing was more evident than the ferocity and courage of our forces at Ross. Their heroism and self-sacrifice were exemplary. We must try to use their struggle to restrict the Titans' movement and their ability to recover and retool."

"The public is starved for good news," said McCall. "Our success at Ross was a shot in the arm, but that was then. This is now, and the recent lack of progress is taking a toll on the citizens' patience. With the presidential election in just a few weeks, we need to be prepared to deal with potential shifts in policy. Much may change then."

Gallant saw the troubled look on Collingsworth's face that reflected his own worry. Both knew what a Neumann victory could mean to the nation, as well as their personal life.

One officer said, "It's important to gauge the enemy's opportunities and failings as much as our own."

The redheaded staff officer said, "We've had many requests to divert resources from military to civilian needs to ease their burden and improve morale."

"I recommend against that approach," said Gallant. "Civilian morale will improve with a victory. Diverting military resources will only hamstring our options."

"But how can we possibly support all five of our star outposts?"

Gallant said, "We have to assess each star system for its strategic value, such as location and natural resources. For example, the Lacaille star system has only a few mineral resources we can't get elsewhere, but its location is critical to our defense."

"What about the new aliens?" asked one officer.

McCall said, "The Chameleon are difficult to fathom, and therefore troubling. SIA is cautious about trusting them, even as we have high hopes about what assistance they might provide."

Collingsworth shot a quick glance at Gallant. "Fleet command is desperate to explore the Great Ship in detail, especially those super-lasers. Their power is awesome. A better understanding of their capabilities would be a huge advantage for us."

Officer after officer expressed concerns. They pointed out that the situation was grave no matter how they looked at it. Preparations for offensive operations were underway on several fronts. The five United Planets' star systems had initiated a massive building program. Battle stations were being constructed in the orbits of key planets. Manufacturing was at an all-time high, producing equipment for ships, fighters, and weapons. Even so, decisive action was not possible with their current strength.

Between the raiders and long-range bombers, the Titans were destroying every merchant ship they could find. The United Planets' merchant tonnage was being replaced as quickly as possible, but it wasn't fast enough.

Admiral Collingsworth stood up and leaned forward, his fists on the table. "Officers, I have heard your concerns before, and I have discussed them with President Kent. He has authorized a new strategic mission."

He turned to Gallant and said, "Captain, present your plan."

Gallant watched their faces as he rose. He knew many of those present were skeptical. Some of them openly disliked and distrusted him.

He said, "I have a map for Operation Damocles—a chart to take us to the greatest treasure in this war—the bombing of the Titan home world, Gliese-Beta."

A murmur of astonishment went through the room.

The redheaded staff officer rose and said, "Admiral Graves has already run extensive simulations for a raid on the Gliese system."

All eyes turned to him. "We estimated that six carriers, six dreadnaughts, and many escort ships, will be protecting the

Gliese star systems and its population of twenty billion. Our analysis team has spent countless hours running simulation and data analysis, exploring such a concept. Our anxiety was never more justified."

He projected a series of assumptions and outcome charts onto the wall viewscreen. He kept up a running commentary as he illustrated the poor results.

The staff officer let the silence draw out. Then he cleared his throat and said, "our conclusion is that such an undertaking would lead to disaster."

Gasps and murmurs emerged.

Everyone's gaze shifted to Gallant. He gave the officer a harsh look, realizing that his authority hung by a knife-edge. He said in a loud, angry voice, "Your work is based on the assumption that achieving the element of surprise would be impossible."

Admiral Collingsworth frowned.

Gallant regretted his loud protest and drew a deep breath. In a more measured tone, he said, "My apologies for speaking so bluntly, but if surprise could be achieved, we would have every opportunity to meet our mission objectives and withdraw in good order with acceptable casualties."

Admiral Collingsworth said, "Captain Gallant makes a fair point."

The staff officer shook his head and protested, "I can see no way to accomplish that."

Gallant clenched his teeth to keep a flood of harsh responses from escaping. The blood drained from his face. Then, as he spoke, he kept any trace of excitement out of his voice, and though each sentence followed without a pause, they did not stumble out but were clearly enunciated in a professional tone.

"My plan for this mission is very different than the simulations you've imagined. It has three key elements. It will begin with a surprise Marine raider battalion crippling a critical Titan defense facility. Then a carrier strike force of starfighters will make a surprise bombing run on Gliese-Beta. They will hit vital but scattered targets to highlight its vulnerability. Finally, a clandestine withdrawal operation will extract the Marines, our starfighters, and our strike task force."

He could see the nodding heads as each military mind began contemplating how they would structure such an attack.

"I can't give you details of this plan now for two reasons. First, we will limit the details to a need-to-know compartmental basis for each separate team. Second, there is a major wildcard remaining that may play a vital role in the mission—the Chameleon."

John Roberts stood. He expected the *Warrior* to play a major part in the operation. He said, "That's more than just a wildcard. It's pure speculation. Before we commit to such a risky plan, we need to know whether they're even willing to help us."

Gallant said, "Their extraordinary stealth technology would be a major asset."

Several heads nodded.

"And if we could convince them to play a role in the mission, their Great Ship could make a dramatic difference in the battle."

Admiral Collingsworth said, "Gentlemen, any help from the Chameleons would be a boon, but this mission is a 'GO' regardless. We must strike a significant blow to the people as well as the leadership of our enemy. This mission is the best way to achieve that."

"I have a general outline of the plan as it pertains to each of you. More details will follow for those who have specific tasks," Gallant said, handing out flash drives with directives.

Ryan scanned his instructions, cleared his throat, and spoke up, sounding a bit nervous. "The coordinates for the bombing launch point are beyond starfighter capabilities, sir."

Gallant nodded. "We're aware of that, Lieutenant. Upgrades to the starfighters are already planned."

Kelsey Mitchel said, "The surveillance specs are likewise beyond current capabilities. Are you planning Hawkeye upgrades as well?"

"If the Chameleon cooperate, we can plan to make stealth upgrades across the board, but we have our own upgrades to make as well."

Lorelei Steward asked, "Our bomb loads are limited, will we make modifications to extend our flight time?"

"You will have additional external tanks for fuel and bomb loads. That is another reason why the improved stealth technology we have already received by the Chameleon will help," said Gallant.

James Steward said, "What size Marine force will be available for a raid on Titan's defense target?"

"I have allocated several specialized Marine raider units for the task. They will be deployed and recovered by a stealth ship. Their participation is critical to getting our starfighter pilots back after the bombing. After the raid, we expect the Titans to scramble every fighter in the star system. Our ships will have been exposed, and no amount of stealth technology will hide them at that time. However, crippling the Titan target I've selected is the key to the mission. The idea is to give those pilots a few minutes' heads start toward our recovery rendezvous without being intercepted by Titan fighters."

Roberts asked, "Rendezvous point?"

"The pilots will eject from their fighters at the rendezvous point ZED and be picked up by the *Warrior*. That's plan B," said Gallant. He leaned forward over the table and added, "Plan A is an option only if we persuade the Chameleons to help."

"What other resources besides stealth can the Chameleons provide us? And what resources do they lack that we can offer in return?"

Gallant said, "They excel at components such as transistors and circuit boards for AI systems, which will be key to our success. I've been working on a scheme to barter with the Chameleons. Items such as titanium, heavy transuranic material, and dark-matter accelerators have piqued their interest. An exchange has already been proposed."

"The Titans may take the Chameleons into consideration."

"Maybe, but remember they've beaten the Chameleons before and no longer consider them a major threat."

"Your proposal is bold, but I'm left with more anxiety than hope," said the redheaded staff officer. "Why have you named this operation, Damocles?"

Gallant smiled, "Because the Sword of Damocles will be hanging over us during this mission. And if we fail to achieve surprise, it will cut our head off—just as you predicted."

CHAPTER 7

Liberty

Liberty call began promptly at 18:00 on Saturday evening, and Ryan was the first one off the Constellation. He took a cab to Milford's best restaurant, filled with positive thoughts and bright hopes, which was the best way to start a date.

As he walked into the eatery, he spotted Lorelei right away, sitting at the bar. She looked stunning in tight jeans and a pale beige blouse. She was sipping from a glass with fruit stuck on the side.

"Sorry I'm late. The local traffic was a problem," he said. "How about you?"

"I grew up in Milford, and I know all the short cuts," she said, nodding to the stool beside her.

As he sat, she smiled, exposing two rows of gorgeous white

teeth. Her long, flowing, red hair lay over her left shoulder, framing her lovely face.

"What are you drinking?"

"A cocktail."

He waved to the bartender and said, "Whiskey, neat." He pointed to the glass in front of Lorelei. "And another one of these."

He said, "You look fantastic."

She blushed happily. "Thank you. It's nice to get out of that baggy flight suit for a while."

"It's been a while since we've had a chance to get away together."

"I know. I'm glad we're here now."

Against the far wall, a four-piece band played rock music, and several couples were dancing.

He shifted his stool closer, and his knee pressed against hers.

"This last year has been insane," he said.

"Do you expect it to get less so?"

He laughed, "No. Not at all. In fact, I think our lives will only get more complicated. That's why I've been reluctant to ask you out."

"Well, I think you've made the right decision."

"In waiting?"

"No. In asking me out," she gave him an alluring smile, fleetingly reminding him of their prior liaison.

A waitress approached and showed them to a table.

"Our specials tonight..." droned the waitress.

Ryan didn't listen. But when Lorelei gave her selection, he said, "Make that two. And bring a bottle of the house wine."

They chatted for several minutes until their meal was brought to the table.

"Is that an endless collection of plates?" he asked.

"No," she laughed as she scooped foods from the various dishes and heaped them on his plate. Here try these."

He looked at the odd-looking dishes and asked, "What is that?"

Lorelei appeared shocked, "Why it's my favorite. I wouldn't come to this restaurant and have anything else. Here."

She took a fork full and held it before his mouth without explaining what was in the concoction.

"That looks... appetizing."

"Yeah," she said and pushed it closer.

He opened his mouth with great reluctance, and she inserted the food.

He began chewing, trying not to gag on the unfamiliar morsel.

"Mmmm. I see why this is your favorite."

He tried to smile and chew while she laughed.

Lorelei finished her meal, which she appeared to enjoy while Ryan lingered over his plate moving pieces of food around with his fork.

After the waitress came by and removed the plates, he said,

"Dusty bet me that you would never date me again."

She laughed. "Kelsey said I should steer clear of you."

"Looks like we don't have a lot of supporters."

"Just us."

Ryan was pleased with that response.

They talked as if it was their first date, filled with conversations about their jobs, their general background, and their families.

Lorelei said, "No one has been left unaffected by the war, in some way. Soldiers and sailors haven't told their families much about what they faced, to spare them heartache. But the families know somehow."

Ryan looked up at her sharply. His childhood had been filled with distress, fighting battles of acceptance as he moved from foster home to foster home. He had been placed in six different homes and separated from those siblings and parents several times. He barely knew them and remained somewhat distant to them to this day.

After a few more drinks, they left the restaurant. Ryan was about to hail a cab when Lorelei said, "Let's walk. I want to feel like I'm home, and that the war is very far away."

They enjoyed the clear, chilly July evening. Looking up, they examined the star-filled southern hemisphere sky. After a while, they stopped and looked at each other.

Ryan licked his lips, leaned forward, and kissed her. A medium kiss, but it escalated. They continued walking for another mile and reached a quaint small-town hotel.

"Can I help you?" asked the clerk.

"A single," said Ryan without looking at Lorelei.

She said nothing, and they went up to the room.

He fumbled with the door, sliding his key card the wrong way, all the while Lorelei kept her arms around his waist. Finally, the door opened, and they were kissing in the middle of the room, standing, leaning against one another—her lips on his neck and then on his mouth.

"Are you drunk?" she asked.

Several uncomfortable moments passed as they stood there.

"No," he mumbled. Because he always said no when he had a few too many. He felt lucid and clear, that was enough. Lorelei was the promise he wanted for himself.

He kissed her again, only this time for a long, long time—not breaking away—not even shifting position. It was an intense, passionate kiss—the kind he wanted to keep sealed in his memory for a lifetime.

The sun poked its red blushing face up over the horizon marking the entrance of a new day and the end of a boisterous night—a night where Ryan had drunk too much and slept not at all.

He dropped his duffle bag next to a tree and sat in the

shadow, staring with bleary eyes at the shuttle that would take him to the *Constellation*. Though it wouldn't take long, he was not looking forward to the trip up to the Melbourne space station.

It was so peaceful on this day that it was hard to believe that the whole of humanity was at war. But the media never let him forget.

News reports seemed to repeat images of Marines lying dead on a barren rock light-years away. The gruesome videos demonstrated all too clearly what words could not express—the horror and pain of war—which most of the populace would never experience firsthand. The dead were far too many. And the war was a constant presence that showed no sign of ending. The bitter reality tested their courage and resolve.

Ryan scanned the area. Everywhere he looked, he saw evidence of the war. On the somber faces of men and women in uniform, among the civilian workers loading weapons from the dockside onto transport shuttles, in the red signs that advertised the emergency shelters. Out of the corner of his eye, he saw the guard towers and munitions warehouses.

Challenging these images were gently swaying trees which pockmarked the area along with lush green lawns. Clouds shackled themselves to the distant mountain range.

He closed his eyes and leaned his head against a tree, trying to extend the sense of calm and relaxation he'd found on leave. He wanted to postpone reporting aboard his ship for as long as possible.

A shadow fell across him.

"Are you ready?" asked Lorelei.

She stood over him wearing a little sweater and tight skirt; her back arched forward, her eyes wide and expectant. The last few days of liberty with Lorelei had been magical. His mind flew back to the previous evening when she pushed herself against him in a bra and pajama bottoms—all passion and lust.

"It's hard to shift gears back to the military after our time together," he said. Not anxious to return to the squadron's problems, he kept his eyes closed.

"I feel the same. It's been a delightful few days."

"Thank you for showing me around. So nice to get a glimpse, even a brief one, of normal life in your hometown."

She shook her head. "Milford is not the same town I grew up in, though. I mean, nothing drastic has changed, at least not on the surface. But how could it remain untouched?"

Both had experienced profound loss while onboard *Constellation* and the experience had given them new eyes. In the same way, Lorelei knew Milford was not what it seemed. Below the surface and in the hidden spaces, the life of her youth was gone.

Ryan said, "The townsfolk we met all feel that they are doing the right thing. They're 'all in' with the service members."

"So many necessities are in short supply. Simple things like bread and butter are hard to get. The people do without, but I've heard lots of talk about 'after the war.'"

'After the war' meant no more food rationing, no more travel restrictions, no more sacrifices that had become routine. It meant new clothes, new fun, a return to laughter. But more deeply, to the families, it meant their loved ones would come home. Children watched through the windowpanes, waiting for their parents. Wives waited for their husbands, mothers for their children. Ryan knew an end to the war meant that life and happiness would return.

She said, "Things will get better. I know they will."

"Where does all that stubborn optimism come from?"

"I believe in the future."

"No, I think it's more than just that."

"Then why do you resist all my suggestions? Why does everything have to be logical and perfect for you to accept it? Why should everything have to be perfect for you to believe in our future?"

With a smile, he reflected on her ability to turn a simple conversation into a loaded discussion about their relationship. "Let me lay out the facts and explain them to you."

"Oh, yeah. Because it's *so attractive* when you explain things to me as if I'm a child."

"You're wrong." He reached out his hand, which she ignored.

"I'm not wrong. I just know my own mind," she said.

He fell silent, reflecting on their quirky chemistry. She was funny, sensitive, and truthful—all qualities he enjoyed—but perplexing and disconcerting as well. He was learning that love, especially his relationship with Lorelei, was seldom as tidy as the starry-eyed anecdotes he had imagined.

She pouted. "Trying to talk to you about your feelings is exhausting. Ask me how I feel, I'll tell you straight up."

"Yeah. I know," he chuckled.

"What does *that* mean?" Her eyes grew wide, and her jaw clenched.

"It means I have a problem understanding you," he said after a moment, failing to find a romantic spin to put on it.

"That's because you don't *want* to. You'd rather not hear my opinion."

"Oh. But you understand me?"

"No, I don't, or at least I rarely do. But I wish I could," she said, furrowing her brow. Her lips pressed into a tight line.

He grinned. "You're funny when you're mad."

She spat, "Your immaturity is appalling." A red-hot scowl flew across her face that matched her hair.

Their flirtation was seriously addictive. He enjoyed the cat-and-mouse game they played, even though he was never sure which of them was the mouse.

"Let's leave the fighting for the Titans," he soothed.

She relaxed a bit. "Okay, sure."

After a few quiet minutes, she added, "Nothing is as easy as it was before. Before us, I mean."

Ryan sighed and took one last soulful look around.

"I guess we might as well report back to the ship."

He heaved to his feet and slung his duffle bag over his shoulder. Together, they walked to the shuttle, disturbed by what they knew lay ahead but ready to rejoin the *Constellation*. The ship was heading out to fight again—battle scars had been healed, repairs made, and lost personnel replaced by eager new faces.

It was not a fight they wanted, but that was not their choice.

CHAPTER 8

Constellation

Gallant had served on many ships over the years but stepping aboard the Constellation always filled him with a surge of pride. He reflected on his last battle with this proud spacecraft carrier and reveled in the Constellation's exceptional fighting qualities.

Too restless to go to his cabin, he strode onto the bridge. Commander Fletcher immediately stood up, waiting for him to speak.

"XO, we have a daunting task ahead of us. Fleet Command has set another arbitrary and unreasonable timetable."

"Yes, sir."

"I need you to establish a work schedule for department heads."

"Huh. Yes, sir. Exactly what items do you wish me to include?"

"First, install the stealth technology upgrades."

He pictured the durable, upgraded low-maintenance stealth technology that used structural fiber material and a quantum field diffusion generator to reduce emissions. There was a new integrated AI sensor fusion system for pilot situational awareness and improved target identification and weapon delivery. The last upgrade was the AI quantum computer for enhanced high-speed data networking supplied by the Chameleon that would double overall efficiency.

"Then we're going to bring an additional twenty-four Viper IIs on board."

"Huh? Where will we find the space to house them, sir?"

"To accommodate them, we will reduce our normal six-month deployment loadout of food, water, and spare parts to two months."

"Even so, sir . . . a single Viper is 20x20x10 meters. That's 4000 cubic meters. Each Viper requires ten times that volume in spare parts and supporting maintenance equipment. That's 40, 000 cubic meters. Also, each Viper requires a team of six support personnel for servicing and maintenance while onboard, plus added crash and fire teams, plus added launch and recovery personnel. Then there is the added food and quarters for the personnel. We're talking about increasing the ship's useful space by several million cubic meters. Do you imagine that I could off-load that much cargo to compensate?"

Fletcher was a good manager with a sharp eye for detail, a little buttoned-up, with her hair pulled back, and her lips pressed together, but Gallant was impressed with her on-the-fly analysis.

He touched her arm and said with a smile, "I have every confidence in your ingenuity, Margret."

"Sir, I..."

"And we will off-load six Hawkeyes."

"Hmm... six Hawkeyes take up... "

He watched as she silently did the math in her head.

"That may do it," she said quietly.

"However, there is one more thing. We'll be adding external missile racks and fuel tanks to all Vipers. I want their travel range doubled, and I want the bombers' payloads tripled."

She said, "The addition of external hardpoints to carry missiles, bombs, and tanks will come at the expense of increased radar cross-section, and thus reduced stealth."

"The external racks and tanks will be ejected when circumstances warrant."

He didn't raise his voice or waste time with niceties. He wasn't angry. It wasn't an argument. It was a discussion. And now they understood each other.

Fletcher's mouth opened and closed several times, but no words escaped.

"I know, I know. Just find a way," he said.

As Gallant turned and stepped into the next compartment, he shouted, "Make a hole."

Several crewmen backed against the bulkhead to make room as the captain squeezed past them on his way to the chief's mess to join them for a cup of sim-coffee.

Within hours, he found crewmen were moving ammunition and supplies.

He should have been pleased with the rapid progress, but the clutter, mess, and disruption to the harmony of the ship annoyed him, and he was upset.

"Blast. Blast!" he muttered and stalked off to the wardroom. Settling into his chair, he looked at the ship's engineer who was sitting with a mug of coffee in one hand and a tablet in the other. They exchanged a few pleasantries, then Gallant leaned forward and put his elbows on the table. "I want to discuss engineering upgrades."

The engineer said, "Of course, Captain. What do you have in mind?"

"In terms of the bomber attack on Gliese-Beta, we need to beef up both the payload and the range of our bombers. The XO is already working on making room for more bombers and external racks. I need you to make starfighter modifications to get those ships in optimal shape."

The engineer took out his handkerchief and wiped his neck. "I'll have to modify the launch rails to accommodate external racks. And putting on extra tanks will increase the danger in the event of a crash."

"I agree. But we must double the range and triple the payloads."

"I'll get on it, sir. I'll need to schedule an extended test period to ensure the mods are satisfactory. What about recovery operations?"

"I've got a plan for recovery that will not require many changes."

"But the external tanks and racks?"

"If we have to recover the starfighters, they will eject them before recovery," said Gallant.

"Still, there is limited space for maneuvering the crafts once they've landed."

"I'm sure you can train landing crews to work that out. Don't be so pessimistic."

"Engineers are paid to be pessimistic," said the grizzled veteran. "Optimism is replete with disappointment."

The talk shifted to technical production needs. The chief engineer outlined what materials and equipment would be required to complete the ship's installations. Next came a discussion on the preparation of missiles and weapons.

Even as they talked, Gallant had trouble focusing. In truth, he didn't know when the mission would happen . . . or whether his ship would be ready.

CHAPTER 9

Everyone Lies

Though Melbourne had a spaceport now, it kept much of her ancestral tradition. She sat at a crossroads, landscaped with small trees and rustic boulders. Forking out from the junction, one of the roads ran to the spaceport shuttle runways in the south. A second ran west toward the mountains. The remaining road angled to the southeast toward the ocean shore, with its high cliffs and many caves.

The city's Royal Botanic Gardens was a popular spot for events, both large and small. In summer, the live theater was a highlight, and a popular picnic spot by a lake was always crowded before performances. The nearby Melbourne Museum sat proudly next to the Royal Exhibition Building and Captain Cook's Cottage.

With its tangle of hidden walkways, tree-lined promenades, and historic Victorian buildings, from the ocean harbors to its spaceport docks, the Gardens offered a welcoming respite for visitors. It also held the seat of the government.

On this occasion, President Richard Kent addressed an outdoor campaign rally.

"You may believe that a nation's army and navy win wars."

He paused, letting his eyes find face after face, making connections.

"But, they do not!"

Spreading his arms wide, he said, "The nation's good people —people like you—are the ones who win the wars. With grit and determination, courage, and fortitude, they prevail by persevering in the face of adversity."

With a firm nod, he added, "And there is no more true character of a nation than those few good men and women who play a pivotal role. The decision one leader makes at a crucial point in battle. The vital bit of information an agent unearths to change the strategy. The factory worker who invents a new and more efficient process that retools the weapons of war! Who are these heroes?"

He looked out over the crowd, pleased to see their enthusiasm rise.

"Who are these everyday heroes who arise in the moment of critical need?" he repeated.

He gazed around the audience again as if searching out the answer from everyone.

"They are you. And you. And you," he pointed. "They are the

people at home who will rise to the occasion as the opportunity presents itself, as circumstances demand, as your nation needs."

Smiling, he said, "This war *will* be won. I have heard your concerns, and in the face of adversity I am hopeful. We will continue to advance."

For all of Kent's eloquence, his presidential campaign was not going well. Titans hit-and-run raids had struck at several United Planets' stars. The news media had a field day criticizing the administration for its lack of preparation and response. Kent was concerned that more bad news might doom his reelection chances.

At the same time, Gerome Neumann took full advantage of the war news to suggest that the military wasn't supporting the president's war plans. Admiral Graves trumpeted the idea at Neumann's campaign rallies. And his political operatives planted stories that even the secretary of defense had lost confidence in military leadership.

Neumann's strategy was convincing people who had been earnest supporters of Kent to turn on one another. He was a master at sowing discord and exploiting the ensuing distrust and confusion.

The Melbourne *Herald* declared:

ALIEN SPIES IN OUR MIDST?

The Solar Intelligence Agency reported a breach of the Planetary Defense AI network and its related databases. The command center in Melbourne was penetrated despite its sophisticated, multilayered security. Within hours reports have come in from around the world of lapses in security, corrupted data, and missing files. Some reports accuse an anarchist terrorist organization, but there is a growing belief that this is the work of alien spies.

At a hastily convened security conference in SIA headquarters, a tall, dark-haired man rapped on the podium for attention. "Good morning, ladies and gentlemen. I'm Special Agent Samuels of the SIA counterintelligence division, and this is Special Agent Maloney. We're part of an interdepartmental investigation into the hacking of our planetary defense facilities. We asked you here because we believe the most likely targets of the breach are ranking members of fleet headquarters, such as yourselves."

Samuels waited for the murmurs of dismay to die down before continuing. "One possibility we are investigating is that this was a terrorist attack. We're tracking some suspicious activity of one special group."

"Terrorists?" asked an officer. "How could terrorists even get past the guards at the gate?"

"Disguises and forged clearances are easy to manufacture,"

said Samuels. "We're not at liberty to release any details yet, but I can tell you that a virus introduced into the security system spread malware. That, in turn, allowed hackers further access."

"Are you considering that aliens may be at the heart of this?" asked a middle-aged woman, scribbling notes in a reporter's tablet.

"The aliens are our primary suspect, given the sophistication required to penetrate the facility."

"What proof do you have?" a voice shouted.

Maloney's face showed no emotion., "This is an ongoing investigation. We are gathering evidence on all possibilities as we speak. Counterintelligence is, after all, called the Great Game. Defensive counterintelligence begins with looking for weak links within one's own organization, assets that could be exploited by foreign intelligence. Counterespionage may involve reactions against foreign services. Many individuals in this room could be considered prime targets for recruitment, or exploitation, by foreign services."

Gallant got the distinct impression that Maloney's gaze lingered on him longer than he would have liked.

Does he think I'm a spy?

Samuels said, "In some circumstances, a simple interrogation could clear up any misgivings. But arrests may be a step in the case of hardened individuals. Once we have a prisoner, he will have the choice of cooperating or face severe consequence up to and including a death sentence for espionage. Cooperation may consist of telling all one knows about the other service. So, if you, or anyone you know, may have been involved, it would be in their self-interest to come forward now."

Gallant asked, "What happened with the guard on duty at the main terminal access point?"

"He told us that he suffered an electrical shock. It disoriented him, and since coming out of a coma, he's been confused, and his memories are vague."

Samuels said, "The trick in espionage is to remember it is a game. The best lies always begin with a convincing truth. The guard could be faking it."

Someone suggested, "Maybe he came upon the intruder, and this is the result of that encounter."

"Possibly, but you can't hide the truth. Truth seeks light.

Gallant sat in the SIA interrogation office, his hands gripping the chair arms as Samuels looked at him with interest.

"My first instinct was to get a warrant to search your home and ship before interviewing you," said Samuels. "You are, of course, one of the more intriguing possibilities to be a spy, given your talents, not to mention your unusual access to high levels in the government. And that is leaving aside your particular close contact with the aliens."

Samuels gave a humorless smile. "Is it possible you disclosed—inadvertently, I'm sure—some security information?"

Gallant took a deep breath and stared at the agent. He placed his hands on the tabletop and said with conviction, "No."

"I don't believe you played a deliberate role in the hack. Perhaps you weren't even aware that you let something sensitive slip. If that were the case, now would be the time to disclose the nature of your conversation. That way we could clear up any, ahh..., misunderstanding."

"No."

"We have found many coincidences," said Samuels, in a patronizing tone, "involving you and the aliens, and access to secure information."

Gallant's gaze didn't waver.

Samuels said, "I can't prove it yet, but I'll tell you what I think."

Gallant felt his chest tightening.

Samuels continued, "I know that you have some special abilities that connect you to the aliens. You also have access to top-level secrets and security protocols. It's been suggested that..."

Samuels locked eyes with Gallant.

Gallant said, "Have you considered that this information may have been fed to you deliberately? Implicating me as a misdirection?"

"Suggested by whom?"

Gallant said, "Those concerns wouldn't by chance have come from Gerome Neumann's campaign headquarters, would they?"

"Ah."

"You mentioned a terrorist organization. Have you examined their involvement?"

"Of course. We can prove that there is an organization bent on anarchy that is involved in hacking activities. Their digital fingerprints have been previously identified at some other, minor facilities. They attempted to cover their trail, including trying to erase the logs, but we saw through that. Yet, we know for a fact that there are no indigenous organizations capable of such a sophisticated hack at the most secure facilities on the planet. No, this attack was unique."

"And that's why you suspect a spy. But why me?"

"Tell me, Captain, have you been having money problems recently?"

Gallant stood up and glared at the agent. Through gritted teeth, he said, "Nothing serious enough to warrant betraying my country."

Samuels didn't flinch. He set a plastic evidence bag on the table between them. "Tell me, Mr. Gallant. Do you recognize this access log?"

Gallant stared at the computer printout. "Is that the time stamp from the hack?"

"It is. Can you identify the entry?"

"It's my access id and password," said Gallant, stunned.

Aurora!

Samuels said, "Only the fact that your fingerprint, iris scan, and facial recognition biometrics weren't accessed gives me pause to arrest you."

He paused for a full two minutes before he said, "That's all for now. Some powerful people have vouched for you. But this investigation will continue, and at some point, I'm sure we'll want to speak to you again. Stay in touch."

CHAPTER 10

President-Elect

Where was the joy?

Winning should have been electric. But rich, powerful, and just elected President of the United Planets, Gerome Neumann, was bereaved of emotion.

He felt empty as he settled back into the plush seat of his limo. He had listened to the news of his upset victory over President Kent with a detachment bordering on indifference. Throughout the campaign, winning had been an abstract concept for him—too elusive to take seriously. But no longer. Now he was waiting for his emotions to catch up with what his mind already knew.

With a smile, he reflected on how he had conquered the political heights and won against all the naysayers and critics. Now he intended to make them pay for their lack of vision and faith.

Catching his reflection in the limo window, he remembered precisely when he had decided to seek the presidency. He was still young and vigorous enough, still handsome, and cut a good figure. His square jaw and prominent chin projected strength and power. It was the look of a man who had built a financial empire in mining and shipping and ruled it for decades. Anyone who got in his way felt the sting of his acerbic tongue and the clout of his immense influence. Yes, he made an excellent candidate.

And now, he had won. Picking up his tablet, he opened the draft of his acceptance speech. What tone should he take—humble and grateful, or proud and aggressive?

He penned a few lines. "I was born in New York City. After taking over my father's successful shipping and mining business, I consolidated them. The company I built was the first major business on Mars. Today, NNR remains the largest industrial complex in the Solar System. It's a major contributor to the war effort, working to keep our citizens safe and prosperous.

"During my career, I've accrued much wealth, power, and influence. Now I welcome this new opportunity. I accept this challenge with enthusiasm. As president of the United Planets, I look forward to demonstrating how one exceptional individual can impose order and structure on a troubled world."

His wife slid across the leather seat and draped her body annoyingly against his.

Why does she always distract me when I'm working?

At forty, Rhea Neumann was still a singularly attractive woman, but she could be an irritating bitch. As his authority had expanded, he had lost patience with her faults. Of course, he had brought his own arrogance and willfulness into the marriage. Still, he had to admit that she often served as a safety valve for the pent-up frustration and rage that occasionally threatened to break out.

None of his failings troubled her because she had convinced herself that she loved him—that his wealth and power had not been the lure that brought her to him. After so many years of marriage, Rhea had developed a shell to wall him off when it suited her. Unfortunately, he seemed to think that meant she had welshed on their agreement that she would support him in all things. While she did what was expected of a business executive's wife, she was boisterous, free-spirited, and too often given to complaining.

Regardless of these shortcomings, two characteristics repeatedly won her back into his favor. First, she was an adroit seductress, and in all their years together, there was never a time he didn't desire her. She was also an exceptional hostess for his many business parties, and he appreciated her flair for lavish entertainment.

Neumann said, "Please be quiet. I'm trying to write my acceptance speech."

Pouting, she pushed him away and leaned forward to turn

on the car's video screen. Neumann was pleased to hear President Kent making his concession speech.

"The people have spoken, and I respect the democratic process. One of the sacred traditions of our politics is that the loser of an election concedes victory to the winner. This facilitates a peaceful transition of power."

Kent waved to his supporters. "I have been blessed to help shape the destiny of our people. I believe I made a difference, and I hope we will find peace soon. I promise you, that time will come, and it's worth fighting for. I look forward to serving my nation in whatever capacity I can in the future."

Rhea said, "Very heartfelt."

Neumann grunted.

Without changing her tone, she said, "Let's bring Kelsey home."

His mind shifted to accommodate her change of topic. He considered his son's widow from an asset and liability perspective.

"She's made her choice. Let her stew in it."

"She's still family. She should be by your side."

For Neumann, Kelsey—like most people—was just another pawn in the complex political game he was playing. Their value was always determined by their use to him. As president-elect, however, he was thinking about Kelsey from a new perspective, colored by her current military assignment. But first, he had some business with ... Henry Gallant.

CHAPTER 11

Hell Week

Captain Gallant felt a surge of pride as he watched the twinkle of the blue-and-gold Marine uniforms coming around the corner at the John Glenn Center on Earth's moon.

Master Sergeant Mike McCauley strode at the head of the battalion.

"Right turrrn... Hut!"

The Marines executed a smart turn in front of the facility. Designed for low-gravity conditioning for special operations, the center featured a transparent geodesic dome that shielded them from the lunar environment.

When they reached the center, the sergeant barked, "Battaaalion... halt! Riiight face!"

Major James Steward stepped forward and saluted Gallant.

"Marine Raider Battalion reporting for duty, sir."

"At ease," said Gallant.

The sergeant said, "Battaaalion . . . paraaade rest!"

With practiced precision, the entire battalion of Marines relaxed into parade rest.

"Your mission is the greatest undertaking in the war to date. To accomplish this mission, you will undergo special conditioning and training. The target is the Gliese star system's fighter command and control center—the very heart and brain of our enemy. You will have no backup and no reserves. If you fail to destroy the center, our entire starfighter force will be annihilated after their attack run. Yours is not a suicide mission, but every decision you make may mean trading your life for the life of those pilots. I don't envy you."

He waited, searching the faces for the faintest flicker of doubt or fear. Seeing none, he continued.

"We have no detailed information on your target beyond its location—a planetoid roughly the size of this moon. The attack plan is based on the expectation that it's like the one in the Ross system. The training you'll receive here will prepare you to cope with the target's potential terrain and obstacles."

He paused again for effect. "This is a voluntary billet, but I doubt if anyone here will turn down a chance to attack the Titan's home planet," said Gallant.

"Am I right?!"

"SIR, YES SIR!!!"

"Carry on, Major," said Gallant, smiling.

McCauley said, "Faaall... out!"

"Grab your gear and head for the barracks. I want your gear stowed, and your weapons serviced before we start. If you had fun in boot camp, then you'll love 'Hell Week.' Now move it. Move it!"

While the battalion collected in the barracks, Steward reviewed Gallant's orders. They detailed his goal of incapacitating a key Titan fighter base centrally located in the Gliese star system. His battalion was to be transported to and from the objective in the stealth ships *Warrior* and *Invidia*. He broke down the mission goal into individual objects for each of his company commanders.

He gathered his officers in the command hut and said, "Each company will have to travel many kilometers on an asteroid to reach their objectives. They must be in peak performance because all four objectives have to be taken simultaneously for the mission to succeed."

At 04:00 the next morning, the battalion was in formation.

"'Hell Week' begins immediately," yelled McCauley. "Let's break it down, Barney-style."

Each face turned to him.

"Every one of you physically perfect Marines will carry 500 kilos of supplies in their backpack. We will march 100-kilometers across the scenic Luna landscape. This march will be the Earth-equivalent of an 80-kilo pack over 40 miles in one day. Trust me, the moon's one-sixth Earth-normal gravity will make the trek a breeze. The sandy, rocky surface is a bonus. Marching with backpacks in light gravity over boulders may produce some bumps and bruises you haven't known before. But don't worry, we'll keep it up until you enjoy it as much as I do."

"Forrrward ... Hut!"

The Marines gave a collective, "Oohrah!" as they stepped forward.

James Steward took the last position in the formation and marched every step with them.

After the first four hours, McCauley stopped and said, "Ten minutes. One sip."

The Marines dropped and took one sip of water. A few minutes later, the march continued.

The modern warriors were equipped with as much high-tech equipment as they could carry. McCauley monitored his people through his augmented reality goggles. He watched their vital signs and physical wellbeing. The AR also gave him a steady stream of environmental data and communications.

At the end of the day, McCauley said, "Drop packs. Two gulps. Go to sleep."

They dropped their packs, took two long-overdue gulps of water, and fell to the ground, instantly asleep. After that first day, the Marines felt almost broken.

Sonny awoke with aches in places he hadn't previously discovered. He cautiously straightened himself; apparently, he slept like a log without changing position and his muscles cramped.

"What day of the week is it?"

Then it all came back to him. It was day two of Hell Week.

He was overjoyed when he discovered they were heading back to base. He couldn't remember a single part of his body that wasn't hurting, except for his arms; those were still numb from the shoulder straps restricting blood flow.

When they reached the gate to the base, McCauley shouted, "Did you like our little walk?"

Sonny shouted back, "No, Sergeant Major!"

"Well, in that case, we'll keep at it until you do."

He ordered the surprised Marines to turn around and repeat the entire journey.

Sonny looked around him at the sea of unhappy faces. "What? What?"

When they arrived at the base for the second time, McCauley shouted, "Did you like our little walk?"

The Marines shouted in unison, "Yes, Sergeant Major!"

"Well, in that case, let's do it again," shouted McCauley in his now raspy 'frog voice.'

Occasionally, some 'smart' guy would try to skate by lightening his backpack. But when McCauley caught them, he added a 'biscuit' (a plastic box shaped like a landmine filled with sand) to their pack.

It didn't get better over the remaining days, but the Charlie company commander challenged the others to a race on the final day. The prize for the victors was a few extra morsels of food and a few extra minutes of sleep. The Marines dug deep, and Able company won bragging rights.

On the night of the seventh day, 'Hell Week' was over. Some members of the team didn't finish with the battalion and had to spend some time in the infirmary to recover.

Afterward, Sonny slept twelve hours straight, then crawled out of bed and went to find McCauley.

"I'm game for this mission, Sergeant. I just want to get my hits in on those Titans. I don't want to die like the guys at Omaha Beach. Two years of training and they drowned stepping off their landing craft without ever firing a shot. I want my life to matter."

"Sonny," said McCauley, leaning in close and speaking quietly, "those soldiers at Omaha Beach mattered, whether they stepped ashore or not. The life of everyone who fights for his home matters."

"Thanks, Sergeant."

Next came the space warfare phase. It concentrated on spacewalk dynamics, space navigation, and small unit tactics while weightless. Hanging onto tethers dragged by jets and falling onto a surface using jetpacks became second nature. Live ammunition exercises were included where they were the targets.

During the final phase, the Marines trained against the replicas of the four Titan base targets. The virtual reality simulations were a welcome respite. Each Marine company had to assault their assigned target and destroy it within the allotted time. Then came breaking through barriers with live explosives and eliminating guards. The exercises were repeated until Steward was satisfied that his team was unstoppable.

He sent a message to Captain Gallant. 'We're ready.'

The message didn't reach Gallant immediately. He was on the Great Ship traveling to the Chameleon's home world in the Cygni star system.

CHAPTER 12

Lord Protector

Walking on the path toward the palace of the Lord Protector, Gallant was astonished by the beautifully sculptured garden. The variety and magnificence of the colorful plants took his breath away only to be matched by the iridescent colors that streaked the sky from horizon to horizon. The color palette was beyond anything Gallant had imagined—an exquisite mosaic that would have made Picasso envious.

The stately palace itself sat atop a sloping hillside outside the capital city, bordered by towering statues carved from what looked like multicolored marble. No doubt, the palace had once been magnificent, but everywhere he looked, Gallant saw cracks and water damage. Age and neglect had taken their toll. Despite its faded glory, its inhabitants carried themselves with pride, as if their ancient grandeur were still intact.

Along the way, Aurora walked beside Gallant, and they fell behind the other members of the Earth delegation.

She spoke softly. "Because the Lord Protector of the Realm suffered from a debilitating childhood illness, he grew up almost unnoticed among the Chameleons' ruling family, which was known for its ruthless scheming and endless lust for power. He spent much of his life in academic study and believed contemplation was preferable to action. As a child, he had an astute tutor who taught him that the Titans killed every Chameleon they found, without mercy or discrimination. He was stunned and repulsed by such violence. His advisor taught him how to handle state affairs with aplomb and skill. Others said it was a mistake to be too generous with praise for lower class people; it raised their stature too much and made them targets for exploitation. He listened as his superiors spoke about matters of state and became skilled in diplomacy. Through the guidance of his tutor, he learned how easily power could slip from the hands of the mighty."

Gallant was surprised at how at ease Aurora seemed to be in discussing her leader's personality and background.

She said, "When his time came to ascend the throne, his appearance was that of a strong-willed man, used to issuing demands and being obeyed. But despite his commanding figure, he was still physically weak. His illness caused many powerful people to underestimate him and seek to take advantage. He was successful in playing his rivals off against one another. And he has exploited the war with the Titans to his advantage by sending his rivals to fight and husbanding his supporters. By the time his enemies realized his potent intellectual and mental strengths, he was too powerful to be challenged. So now his word is law. He is considered stubborn, and he will not listen to pleas of mercy if he thinks he's in the right. He is also perceptive enough to recognize who his enemies are and who his friends are."

"Why are you telling me this so openly?" asked Gallant.

"Because we are approaching a crisis of survival. Both our peoples are on the cusp of an avalanche that may precipitate our extinction. A simple mistake or cultural misunderstanding could benefit the Titans, proving disastrous to us both. I trust that you will be able to help us navigate a safe path through this wilderness."

Gallant hoped that would be true.

Once in the throne room, the delegation stood before the elevated dais where the Lord Protector sat to wield his quasi-monarchical powers. A gallery off to the right side was filled with the republic's parliament.

"Lord Protector," said Aurora with a bow, "here are Earth's representatives." She introduced each member of Ambassador Salinger's delegation in turn, ending with Gallant.

The leader said, "For millennia, the Chameleon people enjoyed a tranquil existence within the lush beauty of our fair planet. Its unspoiled forests, mountains, and streams bred everything we needed for life and comfort. It was where people lived and prospered in peace and happiness until the arrival of the Titans."

Salinger asked, "Are the Titans still a threat to your people?"

"The world of politics is rife with dualities in truth, but when I examine these dichotomies, I find that I savor a unique solution."

Salinger looked puzzled.

Aurora said, "What the 'Father of Our People' wishes to convey is that we are not afraid of the Titans. But we would be pleased to discuss cooperation and mutual security."

Gallant's mind spun through a series of impressions.

Another lie.

Ambassador Charles Salinger served as the primary treaty negotiator. Gallant supported him as an analyst and interpreter. Each day melted into the next as they moved from the early framework to more substantial proposals. They hit a snag when Salinger demanded a guarantee of exclusivity. No separate negotiation or peace agreement with the Titans would be acceptable. Until the Chameleons agreed to that condition, he closed his ears to further discussion.

In the meantime, Gallant pored over documents, seeking to extract every available piece of data. His goal was to learn everything he could about the Chameleon–Titan war. He hoped he would find out about the people's aspirations and motivations.

His own expectations about the mission were clear. While he knew the initial treaty overtures on both sides were tenuous at best, he was struck by the clarity and forthrightness of Aurora's speech. Her openness gave him hope for the eventual success of their negotiations. After all, he told himself, scarcely more than that could be hoped for under the circumstances.

How do we persuade an alien to fight in our war against another species?

CHAPTER 13

Lucky 7

The day was typical.

It didn't involve a morning breakfast at the table with a wife and kids rushing to get ready for school. It didn't involve a commuter train and a ride up the elevator to an office with secretaries and clerks. Those were the activities of civilians in an altogether different world.

This day was typical for a fighter pilot.

First, an engineering tech came into Ryan's stateroom with a detailed status report on his Viper. The 'Lucky 7' was his personal machine. She was beautiful, a miracle of engineering and science with just enough badass to satisfy him. Every curve and angle along her elegant length made him smile. When drifting through space, he would sometimes stroke the control throttles and handles, enjoying the intimate, tactile sense of connection with the machine. In moments of distress, with the ship damaged or malfunctioning, he felt a physical concern in the pit of his stomach. And with every launch, the bond grew.

He believed his sleek Viper made him was more than a match for any Titan pilot in their new multi-winged fighter nicknamed the Phantom. The Viper could accelerate faster and had a smaller turning radius. It was proving to be dominant, despite the Phantom's more powerful laser and plasma cannons.

Ryan completed his flight checks and climbed aboard the sleek craft. The flight chief handed him the checkoff sheet. He was ready for the space wing formation exercises.

Hands clenched on the throttle; Ryan hunched forward. His senses on high alert.

He heard the flight director over his headphones yell, "Launch Viper."

The slingshot launched Lucky 7, and he let out a yell as he flew to join his team.

His eyes scanned the display, focusing on the ships lining up behind him. The fighters began to fill in the open slots in the wing formation in preparation for an extended training exercise. Many of the pilots had not flown together before, and it was essential that they train for the operation ahead.

After twenty minutes, the wing was assembled.

"Twenty-degree roll to starboard," he ordered, settling down to business. "Keep tight through the turn."

The pressure from the g-force pressed against his body as

he absorbed the energy from the turn. Changing the thrust angle, he adjusted the vector.

Under his command, the wing completed several hours of formation flying.

He looked through his display console at the starfighters. Loud and boisterous, Joe Flannery was out of position.

"Bear, you're veering to port."

He pulled up the AI scanner and saw that soft-spoken Samuel Rhodes was misaligned.

"Dusty, stay tight," he admonished.

Finally, he became angry when his own wingman, Glenn Holman, was flying sloppy.

"Duck! Explain how you can be out of position when your wingman to the lead ship?"

"Lucky, how will I ever become an ace, if you're always telling me to stay back?"

A volley of mic clicks sounded over tac1 showing the flight's approval of Duck's question.

Duck got his call sign during training when it was discovered that his antimissiles frequently missed incoming missiles leaving him a sitting duck.

"Lucky. Request permission for bombers to break off for target practice," said Lorelei.

"Permission granted, Flame."

Once Ryan was satisfied with the wing's progress, he ordered them to return to the *Constellation*.

The next day, Ryan walked through the ready room to do it all over again when Lorelei jammed her hands into his chest.

"Rob! You've been drinking," said Lorelei, shock written all over her face. She was stunned that he had smuggled alcohol aboard once again.

"Shhh," he looked around to see if anyone was near. "No, I haven't."

"Don't deny it. I can smell it from here."

"Look, I had one drink. Just to take the edge off. It's no big deal."

"You can't fly like this."

"It's routine training. I could do it blindfolded."

"This is formation training for the raid and requires excellent coordination for your entire team. And you're nearly blind drunk," she said, placing her hands on her hips. "I can't believe you've done this after everything others have done for you."

Ryan felt weird and disoriented, but not exactly drunk. He only had a few drinks over the last hour, but not sober either, just not normal.

"Don't get all dramatic on me. I'm mellow. I fly better when I'm mellow."

He looked around to see if anyone had taken notice of the two of them. He was not concerned, but he wasn't pleased either.

"You turn around now and make up some excuse to go to

sickbay."

"No way."

"Turn around right now."

Somehow his crime came into sharp focus. He felt an impulse to upchuck and dry-heaved over the deck. He sat in a nearby chair, resting his head in his hands and breathing hard through his nose—in, out, in, out.

"I'll never do this again. I'll learn from this. I will. Just let me get away with it this once."

"Ryan, this is not just about you."

"I'm sobering up already."

It was high drama for a minute as dread washed over him.

"Oh, please. I'll never do it again."

"Scratch from this flight, or I'll report you to the OOD as unfit."

"You wouldn't do that."

She looked as if she would cry. "You've given me no choice."

He balled his fists and clenched his jaw. He stood up facing Lorelei for several minutes while he turned beet red.

She stood in front of him unyielding, as determined as he was.

"I mean it," she said.

He sat back down with his hands folded in his lap, waiting for the guilt to wash away.

It didn't.

Is alcohol an excuse? Maybe I'm a bad person.

Finally, he got up and headed for sickbay.

Sitting in her stateroom, Lorelei said, "Rob called me and left a message. It said, 'We should talk about what happened.' I listened to the message several times, but his voice gave nothing away."

Kelsey sighed and gave her a hug. Her heart sank. "What is there to talk about? What is there to say? You can try the avoidance method."

For a moment, Lorelei recalled their time on liberty. And their time in bed. She thought he was a lover without a flaw. As if he had cast a spell over her.

She said, "He told me that was the only time he got drunk before a flight."

"Do you believe him?" Kelsey frowned.

Their eyes locked.

"Lying is his strong suit," admitted Lorelei. "What would you have done?"

"Would you like to know?"

"I would actually. Tell me."

"I'm not sure. Same as you, I guess."

"What are you thinking?"

"Is he even your type?"

"What do you think this is a high school cafeteria?" asked Lorelei. "I don't know if I even have a type. My dating history is checkered. I've only dated a few men. The most serious was a commercial pilot named Jake. He gave me a tingly feeling the first time we met."

She sighed. "We were volatile in bed, but all that heat carried over into screaming matches about the most trivial things. It ended with 'we'll always be friends.'"

Kelsey gave her a sympathetic look.

Lorelei said, "I'm afraid that's how Rob and I will end up."

CHAPTER 14

Treaty

Once the delegation had assembled in the Chameleon conference room, McCall demanded, "Give me all your personal devices."

Salinger and the delegation team placed a treasure trove of tablets and comm pins on the table.

Gallant began examining them one at a time. He used his AI security software to run scans.

"I've already checked my devices. They were clean," he said.

It took over an hour before he concluded, "These are clean as well."

"That's it, then?" asked McCall

"Not quite. Now we need to check your spy drones and the data you collected while you were here."

McCall hesitated for a moment to reveal her nefarious

activities. But finally, she logged on to the 'baseball' drone and downloaded its contents.

Gallant spent another hour tediously sifting through the data, and the software looking for malware of any kind.

He concluded, "Nothing."

McCall said, "I would have been surprised if you found anything. I spent several days last week adding an additional security layer to my drone spyware."

"We can't be too careful, given the current circumstances," said Gallant.

"Yes. I agree," said Salinger. "Does this mean the Chameleon aren't spying on the delegation?"

McCall said, "No. It just means they haven't penetrated our personal devices. I assume that our quarters are bugged and that we're under scrutiny wherever we travel. This room is only safe because Captain Gallant and I swept it and removed a bug before we assembled here."

Salinger said, "As we proceed with negotiations, I want everyone to be conscious of the possibility of being under observation. We will do periodic sweeps for bugs. We'll keep our secrets only by carefully protecting the negotiations points we are will to trade before making concessions with the Chameleon."

After several weeks, Ambassador Salinger was satisfied he had two treaties that he could take back to Earth for ratification by the United Planets' Senate. The first was an alliance that included the two species' core values and goals—a mutual defense strategy to end the war with the Titans.

He was especially pleased with the second agreement, which addressed commercial trade, passports, and immigration.

Gallant read through Salinger's draft documents. The treaty articles pledged to honor each nation's claim to its current planets. The United Planets assured support to evaluate Chameleons' claims to planets overrun by the Titans and agreed to apportion any planets captured in future battles equally. And they pledged to preserve each nation's liberty, sovereignty, and independence. With all their discourse about such crucial issues, though, the documents were modest in scope and short on details.

The Chameleons had made no secret of their desired outcome. But Gallant knew that hopeful expectations could be a great vice. After the preliminary treaty was accepted and signed by Aurora, she was made minister plenipotentiary and the sole Chameleon representative to the United Planets.

THE TREATY OF ALLIANCE

Upon ratification by the governments of both parties, the parties agree to the following:

> Article 1: A military defense alliance will be formed between the Chameleons and the inhabitants of the United

Planets, binding each respective military force in efforts for the direct purpose of maintaining the liberty, sovereignty, and independence of United Planets and the Chameleons.

Article 2: Joint military ventures against an aggressor, the Titan Empire, will be a product of mutual agreement.

Article 3: Technology transfer between the two nations will be through mutual negotiations between the parties.

Article 4: Each party affirms that they will not seek a separate peace with the Titans. Each will divide equally any lands obtained from the Titans through successful military campaigns, or concessions made by the Titans, in peace treaties to end hostilities with the signing nations. The United Planets agree to share control of any land it can gain possession of.

Article 5: This alliance is approved and authorized in perpetuity.

In addition, they agreed to a treaty of commerce. It promised to recognize the property rights and promote commercial ties between the two nations.

Almost immediately after the signing ceremony, Salinger began to question the virtue of a perpetual alliance.

For Gallant, the greatest satisfaction came when he convinced Aurora to have the Great Ship take part in the raid on Gliese-Beta. She agreed to have the Great Ship be at the required coordinates at the specified time to recover the United Planets starfighters.

Despite his elation over this agreement, he wasn't blind to the potential pitfalls.

CHAPTER 15

Diary

Homecoming was always a tremendous source of joy and relief. When Gallant returned to the Melbourne spaceport, Alaina was waiting for him. He never let himself relax until he saw her in person and knew she was safe and happy after being alone for so long. He was aware that she had her own anxiety about him, but he always dismissed the dangers he faced.

"I missed you," she said, giving him a warm hug and a kiss.

"I missed you, too. You look terrific. Any problems while I was away?"

"I'm fine, but the world changed while you were gone."

He stared into her troubled eyes.

"Gerome Neumann took office," she said, erupting with an ugly truth. "He immediately sent congress legislation to enforce new genetic engineering laws. All driver's licenses, passports, job applications, immigration permits, school applications, will now require the user's genetic engineering profile. Even voter registration is included."

"I doubt that will pass the legislature."

She stomped her foot in frustration. "Don't you understand! He's trying to make Naturals into second-class citizens. That violates civil rights, and lawsuits will be filed around the world."

Gallant said, "The public will never accept it. People should be judged on their abilities, not their heritage. There will be pushback against the Genetically Enhanced.

"These laws will change our lives. Do you know what the GEs see when they look at you and me?"

She waited for a second before answering her own question.

"Nothing. They see nothing. We're nonentities hardly worth regarding."

"Don't become upset. We'll survive. Our kind has always survived," he said.

"I want to believe that. I need to believe that."

By the time they reached their apartment, she had calmed down, and they returned to more personal topics.

She beamed with pride as she added, "I got my article published. See here."

He looked at her tablet.

"I'm so excited about my new job with the Melbourne *Herald!*" She beamed with pride as she flipped through several screens. "I got my first article published, with a byline and everything. See here? 'Our New Friends, The Chameleons.'"

Before he had time to read more than the headline, she continued, "Anything can be news, but not everything is newsworthy. Journalism requires both storytelling and verification to make it meaningful. I interviewed Captain McCall and several other people she recommended."

"How did that go?"

"Julie Ann was generous with her time and gave me lots of background material even though she wouldn't let me use her name. I included her information as from 'an unnamed SIA official.' As a journalist, I have the responsibility to conduct in-depth research into every story—identifying sources, fact-checking all my information. She's the one who gave my article the authenticity it needed for my editor to release it."

Gallant pictured the two women facing each other across a table, eyes locked, talking about . . . him. He tried to block the image, not wanting to imagine what thoughts they exchanged.

"Congratulations. I'm proud of you. This took a lot of initiative and perseverance."

She smiled. "Let's go out to dinner to celebrate. A welcome-home feast."

"Sounds great, let me grab a quick shower and change into civvies."

Stripping off his uniform, he stepped into the shower, letting the hot soapy water soothe his muscles. He lingered, enjoying the pleasant sensation that was so restricted on the ship, before finally turning the water off and grabbing a towel. After rummaging through the closet for fresh clothes, he sat on the bed to dress and noticed Alaina's diary on her dressing table.

Without thinking about it, he began thumbing through the screens, even as his conscience rebuked him for invading her privacy. He was pleased at first with what he read.

She loved him. He was the man she wanted all her life. Her words of love and warmth wrapped around him like a blanket.

But then he read several troubling entries, describing her fears that he might leave her for another. His past relationship with Kelsey gave her doubts about his loyalty and commitment to her.

Gallant could scarcely believe what he was reading, but her concern was obvious—and that worried him. He wondered, could she be interested in someone else? His heart had been hurt before, and he didn't want to lose her. She gave his life meaning, but he didn't know how to reassure her.

He gave a guilty start at the sound of her footsteps.

"Henry, are you ready?"

She stopped cold in the doorway and stared at her diary in his hands.

"Just a minute," he said, closing the tablet with a snap.

She hesitated a moment, then came into the bedroom and

picked up her hairbrush. Running the brush through her hair, she took a deep breath and looked at him in the mirror.

"Well, Henry?" Her voice was sharp; the hurt evident.

"I'm so sorry. I didn't mean to, but it was just lying there, and ... I just couldn't resist peeking," he said, hanging his head.

"You shouldn't worry about Kelsey. That's all in the past. Nothing will ever happen between us."

"Really?! There must be a reason why she's still a part of your life," she said, her voice rising. "Did you ever wonder what it would be like if she had chosen you instead of Anton? If you had held on to her?"

He searched for words to make it better. "That's a lot to think about in a few seconds."

"Maybe that's just the right amount of time to not overthink it." Alaina turned away to hide her tears. "You want everything to be orderly and logical. You want to make a column of pros and cons, total it all up and find the answer of who to love in an equation. That's not real life. You have emotions, whether you want them or not. Life is *messy*. And sometimes it hurts."

CHAPTER 16

Secrets

President Gerome Neumann stood next to his rosewood desk in his expensive, perfectly tailored suit; he was a dominating presence—tall, fit, and still young-looking for his years. In contrast, his drawn-down eyebrows and twitchy mouth suggested a scheming, manipulative personality.

He sat and began drumming his fingers on his desk. One of his new favorite activities was watching the high-ranking military leaders of the United Planets parade before him.

"Come forward, gentlemen," he said, flexing his hands.

In a rich baritone voice, he said, "Today, we face serious threats, both external and internal."

He paused for dramatic effect. "The Titans have plagued us for years, and now these mysterious Chameleons are an unknown entity."

Inspecting each face in turn, he fixed each officer with a cold stare. He was expecting a complicated chorus of voices expressing differing opinions, but none spoke up.

"I am dissatisfied with the Chameleon treaty. It's vague and nonbinding and relies completely on good-faith efforts. I don't trust them. They've kept too many secrets from us." He hesitated, considering his own experience with and understanding of secrecy. He knew that people who learn the secrets of others often wind up dead, but those who fail to uncover hidden threats are also vulnerable.

Collingsworth said, "They have offered support for our Gliese-Beta raid."

Graves scowled. "Kent's dream raid is foolish, a suicide mission. It's a complete waste of men and material on a hopeless errand without any real strategic significance. Any attack from us will be nothing more than a pinprick to the Titans. They will wipe out every member of Task Force 34 and hardly notice."

Graves stared at Gallant, daring him to speak.

Neumann faced Gallant and raised an eyebrow. Savoring his success and power, he was aware of how easy it was for politicians to think they were fooling others, only to find, in the end, that they had fooled themselves. Unknown factors and unforeseen possibilities made him cautious.

Gallant said, "While the proposed raid will likely have only a minor tactical impact on the Titans' war machine, hitting the home planet of Gliese will have a significant effect on the morale of their population. Their leadership will be forced to shift significant forces to defensive operations. This will give us an opportunity to move in on other star systems."

Neumann viewed the war with the Titans as a mere backdrop to his own political opportunities. He was confident he knew who his friends were, but still, he looked to the future with a sense of unease. If the Gliese raid was a suicide mission, then he was content to send Gallant. If it was doomed to failure, then it was Kent's failure, and Neumann would bear no blame for it. On the other hand, if it succeeded, he would benefit. He saw only upside for himself.

SMACK!

He slapped his hand on the table.

The drumming stopped abruptly. He said, "I will authorize the plans for a raid on Gliese-Beta. It will be a good test of the Chameleons' earnest intentions. We will see if they fulfill their promises."

It's possible that government groups are already working against me.

What vexed him most about the presidency was that he had to rely on others to carry out his orders. Orders that he gave in excruciating detail only to find them haphazardly executed. An occasional error of judgment might, under someone else's implementation, lead to dangerous repercussions that his money and position could not overcome. His eyes flicked around the room again. In the back of his mind, he always kept the memory of his misdeeds. Self-doubt poisoned his thinking and led him to mistrust everyone around him.

Giving his head a small shake to clear his thoughts, Neumann added, "But we must also confront a more insidious, internal threat to our republic. An existential threat—one that President Kent chose to ignore—popular unrest against genetic engineering. I ran on this issue and dealing with it is one of my top priorities."

They waited to see how Neumann would address this issue.

"I'm creating a special all-volunteer military branch to act as my proxy in facing any unruly behavior to the new genetic engineering laws I have proposed. I intend those laws to be enacted soon and implemented by this GE militia."

CHAPTER 17

Cruel Business

Captain John Roberts stepped aboard the UPSS Constellation CVS-647 as she orbited over Earth to report to his senior officer. He walked into the luxurious stateroom and glanced about him. It was the first time he met Gallant in the captain's formal stateroom rather than his tiny cabin off the bridge. The comparison was startling. The spacious living room was connected to an adjoining suite of bed and bath. There were stuffed chairs and lounges for entertaining political figures and senior officers while in port. The lavish furnishings included paintings, carpeting, and viewscreens. He heard soft opera music playing in the background.

Roberts frowned as he walked toward the adjacent study and eyed Gallant critically. He looked as tall and gangly as the first time they had met, but his uniform was disheveled, he needed a shave and appeared as if he hadn't slept in days.

Though it occurred to Roberts that a remark about his friend's untidy appearance was warranted, he held his tongue because, for those who served, military friendships were special. They acknowledged that they faced dangerous struggles together and that their time on Earth was brief.

The study was sparse and could have used a coat of paint. The only thing hanging on the wall was a viewscreen. Several bookcases were loaded with computer printouts, documents, and miscellaneous devices. The disarray extended to the deck, which was also obstructed with piles of charts and blueprints.

Roberts assumed that the voluminous paper must be battle plans for the upcoming operation. But as he neared and glanced at them, he realized they were not combat studies at all. They were detailed ship layouts and storage data along with miscellaneous personnel records.

He furrowed his brow. Surely, such matters were better left to the XO and not worthy of the time of a Commodore about to embark on a critical war mission.

He took a step closer and cleared his throat, "Ahh, . . . Henry?"

Startled, Gallant sprang up, scattering dozens of documents off his desk and onto the deck. He looked down at the papers as if they had betrayed him. He sighed and began picking them up, trying to place them in their original order.

"Logan! Logan," he yelled.

Rather than walk through Robert's side of the cramped office, which was relatively clean and well-organized, Midshipman Daniel Logan traversed the path from the connecting computer room to the captain's desk like a soldier passing through a minefield.

"Yes, sir?" he panted.

"I've updated the ship's reload specifications. See that the XO gets the storage and personnel reassignments."

The midshipman gazed at the pile of papers. His eyebrows went up, and his mouth dropped open. "Gosh, sir, I don't know ...,"

Gallant selected several printouts full of red marks and notations. He handed them to Logan. "Update the database with these and give the XO a file copy. She'll know what to do."

"Oh. Yes, sir," said the young man grasping the papers. "I mean, aye aye, sir,"

Before he could move, Gallant said, "And be quick about it!"

Roberts was surprised that he snapped at the midshipman. But he attributed it to exhaustion and not that he intended to be cruel or to embarrass the young man.

He was proven correct when Gallant relented and spoke softly, "Sorry to push you so hard. Your outstanding performance in running the necessary studies has been invaluable. I don't know what I'd do without you."

Logan paused and took a minute to digest the unexpected compliment.

"Thank you, sir. That's thoughtful of you. I appreciate it."

Gallant immediately shrugged it off to avoid any show of sentimentality.

The midshipman ran from the study, his arms flailing about to keep from dropping the documents.

Roberts saw a twinkle in the depth of Gallant's melancholy eyes.

Extending his hand, Gallant said, "Welcome aboard, John. Have a seat. No, not in here, everything is a little..., ahh,... precarious. Let's sit in the other room."

Roberts asked, "Are you getting enough sleep?"

"I'll get plenty once we go into warp," said Gallant. Leaning forward with his jaw jutting out, he said, "For now, every detail I fail to complete could mean harsh consequences for the task force later."

Roberts remembered that Gallant was at his best when the pressure was the greatest. Feeling a brotherly impulse, he said, "Still, you shouldn't run yourself ragged. You should delegate as much as possible to the XO."

"Quite right."

They sat in awkward silence for a minute.

"John, did I ever tell you about the initial conversation I had with my first commanding officer?"

"No, I don't think so."

"Captain Kenneth Caine was fastidious with his appearance—clean-shaven, with close-cropped hair and an immaculate uniform. He was just as exacting with the *Repulse*. She was a tight, well-disciplined ship. When I reported aboard, he asked me to describe the ship's mission, which I did. Then he asked me, 'What is the single most important element in achieving victory?'"

Roberts leaned closer.

"I returned his stare, clenched my jaw, and with all the vigor a seventeen-year-old could muster, I spit out, 'surprise, sir.'"

Roberts grinned.

"Well, I participated in the 'Battle of the Asteroids.' It was designed as a grand scheme by the Titans to catch us by surprise, but Admiral Collingsworth turned that on its ear and surprised them instead."

"I happen to know you had something to do with that," said Roberts.

Gallant smiled. "One of the earliest accounts of an epic surprise attack is the Greek legend of the Trojan Horse. The story goes that in a ten-year war between the Greeks and the Trojans, the Greeks finagled a way to get a large wooden horse inside the city of Troy. Hidden inside was a force of Greek warriors who emerged and opened the city gate, allowing the Greeks to defeat the Trojans."

"What's your point?"

Gallant said, "You're going to be my Trojan Horse. You and *Invidia* will transport a Marine battalion to an asteroid deep in Titan territory."

"That's many hundreds of men more than our ships can

accommodate."

"Accommodate comfortably, you mean. And you're right about that. But this won't be comfortable. You'll need to offload spare parts, extra food and water, nonessential personnel, anything that isn't nailed down."

Roberts said, "Even with all that, the Marines will be packed like sardines. Besides the extra bodies, we must accommodate their weapons and assault gear plus their food requirements. We'll have to offload our *Wasp* craft and even some of our personnel."

Gallant chuckled as he pointed to the heap of printouts on his study's desk. "I found a way. Use your imagination. I'm confident that you'll find a way as well."

His raised eyebrow acknowledged their mutual burden; then he launched into the most detailed blueprint for equipment and personnel storage that Roberts had ever heard.

He's brilliant. Seeing his plan is like being inside a supercomputer.

"I'm grateful for your advice," said Roberts finally. "I'll get right on the modifications."

He asked, "Are you feeling all right?"

Gallant sighed and nodded, "I'm fine."

A knock on the door interrupted the pair.

A Marine guard peeked in and said, "Captain Turnbull is here, sir."

Gallant rose and said, "Come in, Captain Turnbull. I'm

pleased you could come. Please have a seat. Can I fetch you a beverage?"

Admiral Graves' chief of staff gave Gallant a perfunctory handshake and took a seat. "No, thank you. I'm glad I could have a few minutes of your time. I wanted to get caught up on your operational plan."

She turned her round red face toward Roberts, and added, "I'm glad you're here as well, Captain Roberts."

Turnbull cast a disdainful look at Gallant's appearance, then with a haughty stare, she locked eyes with Gallant. The tension in the room intensified.

Roberts thought she was not only a captain but a direct liaison to the Third Fleet commander. She can say what she likes, and he doesn't get to not like it.

Gallant spoke carefully. "Let me give you a rundown of the timetable. *Warrior* and *Invidia* will enter the Gliese star system at D-day minus 14. They'll travel into the asteroid field and set up two battery charging stations. Task Force 34 will remain on the outer edge of the system and sending out drones and Hawkeyes to do surveillance. We'll get a fix on their home fleet position and fighter bases."

He traced his finger on the viewscreen along the intended path.

She said, "You are deliberately sending your task force into a star system where you know a more powerful fleet exists, but you have no advance intelligence where it might be located. Is that correct?"

"Captain, I acknowledge that is the case, but I am confident that we can reduce our risk through strong drone and Hawkeye search patterns. We will discover the home fleet position and the location of hidden sensor arrays before they can become a threat."

The heavy-set woman narrowed her eyes at Gallant, her lips pursed. "You're leaving a lot to chance."

"A calculated risk-reward equation with the ability to assess and adapt," was his reply.

Turnbull said, "I will be keeping a detailed record for Admiral Graves' review."

Roberts saw that this would be irritating and a hard pill to swallow. She would be Gallant's cross to bear.

Gallant continued, "On D-day minus 3, Roberts will land the Marines on the far backside of the fighter base asteroid. Major Steward will travel for three days to secretly reach his attack position on D-Day."

"That fighter base must be neutralized, or it will be a major threat to our returning starfighters after their raid on Gliese-Beta," added Gallant. "The *Warrior* will have to wade through enemy forces to extract the Marines afterward."

Turnbull said, "That's a tough job and a tougher schedule, even assuming the *Warrior* can maintain maximum stealth at all times."

"It's no worse than the space wing will face in attacking the Gliese home world," said Gallant. "Timing will be critical. The

Marine assault must begin just as the starfighters start dropping bombs."

Turnbull asked, "How will the task force operate during all this?"

Gallant said, "After we launch the starfighters, Task Force 34 will make a diversionary attack on the outer planets to draw the Titan home fleet away. When the starfighters reach Gliese-Beta on D-day, Steward will already be assaulting the fighter base."

She said, "What about their extraction?"

"Once Steward has knocked out the Phantom base, the *Warrior* will swing back to the asteroid and pick up the Marines. Hopefully, the Great Ship will be at point ZED to drop cloak and recover the starfighters. Then we'll all get the hell out."

"Your plan sounds not only risky but volatile. Almost any hiccup, and there'll be hell to pay."

"I can't deny that. War is a cruel business. Still, it's worth the gamble," said Gallant with a grim expression.

"I hope you're right because I'll be right there with you," said Turnbull. "On Admiral Graves' direct orders."

Gallant and Roberts exchanged glances. "In what capacity?"

"Since Task Force 34 is part of Admiral Graves' fleet, I'll be there to advise you. He has found me to be a stalwart chief of staff, offering valuable counsel, and wants my evaluation of your campaign. However, I am willing to take the role of an observer if that arrangement makes you more comfortable."

"I will welcome your suggestions, Captain," said Gallant, but the corners of his mouth turned down.

Roberts hid a smile. He trusted Gallant, knew he wasn't merely competent but possessed a level head, cool judgment in a crisis, and the ability to innovate contingencies when needed. He said, "No one else will judge Gallant more harshly than he judges himself."

CHAPTER 18

Operation Damocles

On D-day minus 14, the Constellation collapsed its warp bubble on the outer edge of the Gliese-581 system. The task force moved through normal space in a spherical formation with the carriers in the center, the battle cruisers above and below them, and the cruisers and destroyers making up the outer perimeter of the sphere. It was the opening move of Operation Damocles.

From his command chair, Gallant scanned the sensors and surveillance readouts. Some of the light reaching the *Constellation* was several days old, but he didn't suspect much had changed in that time.

The sensor operator reported a busy planetary system teeming with ships moving between five planets. The M-class red dwarf was smaller and had less mass than Sol, which was 20 light-years away."

The helmsman reported, "Sir, we're three light-days from the Gliese sun. There are five planets visible. The nearest to the star is a composite of metal-rich rock over a barren volcanic mantle. Gliese-Beta is the second planet, and both are within the liquid methane zone. It has one large moon, and it's wrapped in a hydrocarbon smog suspended in a nitrogen-rich atmosphere."

The XO said, "There are many mining colonies, military bases, and communications satellites throughout the system. There must be billions of aliens and thousands of ships. The traffic is terrible."

The sensor operator continued, "The third planet has a dense climate. The last two planets are gas giants with several moons like our Neptune."

Gallant ordered surveillance drones and Hawkeyes into the system to find areas of minimal activity where they could skulk without being discovered. He sent stealth drones to infiltrate the system and locate the Titan fleet. He dispatched a Hawkeye search group to uncover hidden system detection arrays.

Gallant told the OOD, "Please ask the XO to join me on an inspection tour in the operations compartment."

He only had to wait a few minutes. Fletcher came through the hatch and said, "Good day, Captain."

"Good day, XO. I want to see if we are still space worthy after the transit."

"Of course, sir. I've made routine inspections since we left.

I have a long list of modifications that are already underway. I'm shifting supplies as usage frees space."

"Good. Good."

"May I suggest we start with the crew's quarters, they're restless under the restrictions."

Gallant followed the XO into one of the packed compartments.

As he went through the hatch, the below decks watch petty officer was about to call 'attention on deck,' when Gallant said, "As you were."

There were over fifty men and women in the compartment, some still in their bunks, others in their skivvies washing up or packing up their belongings. The cool air blowing into the compartment carried a faint tang of motor oil. It fought against the hot body odors that assailed Gallant's nostrils. Slight echoes from multiple conversations bounced off the walls throughout the space. The din remained undiminished as he moved past individuals.

He was met with surprise and occasionally with skepticism as he inquired about their well-being.

"How are you getting on?" he asked one woman.

She sighed, "As best I can."

He was aware that they were all making do under the unpleasant circumstance.

The inspection found every nook was loaded with supplies and equipment, and the crew was frustrated. They had difficulty finding the tools and equipment they needed to do their jobs. He got an earful of complaints, all of which he referred to the XO.

Returning to the bridge, the one place not filled with clutter, he pulled up his orders on his viewscreen.

From: Commander-in-Chief, United Planets Fleet

To: Commodore Henry Gallant, UPSS *Constellation* CVS-647

Subj: Operation Damocles

Ref: (a) BuPers Order UP 067009 (b) Task Force (c) Timetable

Conduct operations in hostile territory as Reference (a).

Commodore Gallant to lead Task Force 34 as per Reference (b).

Attack Titan planet Gliese-Beta as per Reference (c).

George Forsyth Collingsworth

Fleet Admiral George Forsyth Collingsworth

Commander-in-Chief, United Planets Fleet

Reference (b) Task Force 34

2 Spacecraft Carriers –

Constellation, Courageous

Starfighter Space Wing

72 Viper I,

96 Viper II,

12 Hawkeye

2 Battlecruisers – *Indefatigable, Indomitable,*

12 Cruisers

48 Destroyers

2 Stealth Recon – *Warrior, Invidia*

Reference (c) Timetable

D-6 *Constellation, Courageous* launch star fighter wing

D-3 *Warrior, Invidia* land Marines on target asteroid

D-day

- Starfighters attack Gliese-Beta

- Marines attack Titan fighter command

- Task Force acts as Decoy

D+2 *Warrior, Invidia* extract Marines

D+3 Starfighters rendezvous at ZED with the Great Ship

Gallant considered his senior task force officers. He knew Captain Ramsey of the *Indomitable* and Captains Hernandez of the *Invincible* from their performance in the Ross star system. But he hadn't met Captain Jackson of the *Courageous* before she joined the task force.

He asked, "XO, do you know Captain Jackson of the *Courageous*?"

Fletcher said, "Not well, sir. All I know is that she was a favorite of Admiral Graves. I'm surprised he parted with her for this mission. However, she is renowned for her unbridled courage."

Gallant was pleased that the XO had favorable words. He would have to count on her when tough decisions were needed.

Fletcher said, "Our task force will face severe challenges. I hope the plan is adaptable enough to meet them."

"It's a good plan," he muttered. "It *will* work."

The XO leaned over, skimmed the orders, and said dryly, "How many times have you seen a good plan fall apart? Especially when the enemy holds all the cards."

"Not all the cards," said Gallant. "We still have the element of surprise."

Gallant was expecting the knock on his cabin door.

"Enter."

"Lieutenant Ryan, reporting as ordered, sir."

"At ease. Have a seat, Lieutenant."

Ryan sat on the only available chair in the room.

"It's almost time to begin Operation Damocles."

"I'm ready, sir."

"Are you? I've placed a great burden on your shoulders. As wing commander, you'll have to make tough decisions—decisions that will affect many lives—the lives of your pilots, and the lives of those in the task force which may suffer as a result."

"I know that, sir. And I'm proud that you had the confidence to select me for this post."

"You are an expert pilot and a natural leader. Pilots want to follow you. You have an innate sense of duty and responsibility. But to be honest, I've wrestled with the decision to put you in command of the wing."

Gallant saw a great deal of himself in Ryan—an internal voice that pulled him in divergent directions over difficult choices.

"You have made some poor personal choices in the past. I hope you've learned from that."

Ryan's troubled face showed his difficulty in sorting through Gallant's description.

"I have been slow to learn some of life's lessons, but I can assure you that I have. I won't be the cause of failure in this mission," he said that as earnestly as he could.

But in the back of his mind, he was thinking how close he had come to failure only days before. Silently he promised himself he wouldn't let Lorelei, or anyone else, down.

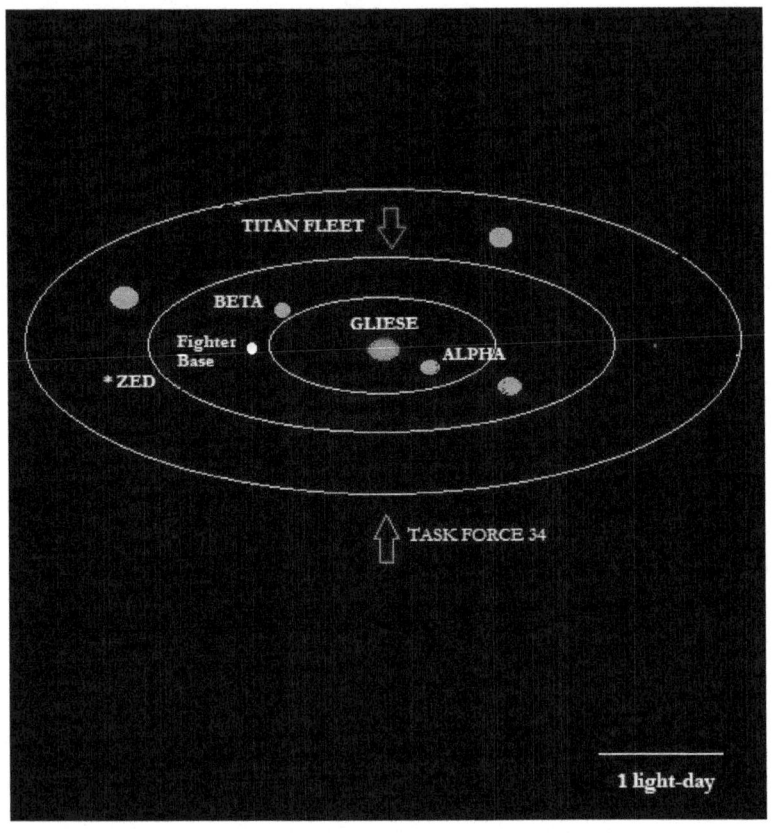

GLIESE Star System

CHAPTER 19

Trojan Horse

On D-14, the Warrior and the Invidia dropped out of warp at the edge of the Gliese star system. Like the huge wooden horse that concealed Odysseus and his men inside, the ships' bellies bulged with Marines. And just like the Greeks who crept out of the horse and opened the gates for the rest of the Greek army, Steward's Marines would unleash their own surprise.

But waiting inside the belly of the Trojan Horse was no joke.

The *Warrior* had gorged herself fully. She was so overpacked that there was no place to stretch one's legs without pushing against another. Her burden of men and material was far beyond the ship's original design, and the makeshift alterations were proving problematic. The sailors needed enough room to carry out their duties, which forced the Marines into not only tiny quarters. But limited free space for ordinary movement. A certain amount of hustle and excitement was routine but always confined to a small space.

Steward had never been claustrophobic. He had never experienced anxiety or fear of confined spaces. But his journey aboard the *Warrior* was the most unpleasant traveling experience he had ever endured. He was a veteran with many years' service, but this ship stank. The smells and noises in the cramped spaces caused him to sweat, experience occasional shortness of breath, and become lightheaded.

He slept in a hammock two meters long, one meter over the deck with two hammocks swinging above him. They were packed together in tiers and slept in shifts. His spine was slow to adjust to the curvature, but he learned to turn over without fully waking up. At daybreak, his mind was still clouded by sleep. Often, he woke in an overheated condition with puke on the deck around him. He would remain in his hammock long after reveille because each morning, it was a chore to use the washroom. Showers were off-limits because they were full of supplies. Washing in a sink had to be accomplished in shifts.

Cooking, preparing, and distributing food made meals another difficulty making the *Warrior* a less than happy ship.

Despite the difficulties, every day, Steward pulled out his personal gear from a mound of battalion storage to clean and service his weapons. He meticulously replaced them since he considered this was a matter of pride that he would not forego under any circumstance.

Exercise was impossible, and there was limited opportunity to escape from the day-in and day-out hot, smelly people around him. He knew this was true for everyone on board, but that didn't make it any more tolerable.

On one occasion, he was allowed onto the bridge to discuss deploying his men when they reached the asteroid. He spoke to Roberts for as long as he could to prolong his stay in the relatively spacious bridge area. He was treated to a splendid view on a monitor as Task Force 34 moved through space.

It was a magnificent display of cruisers and destroyers led by battlecruisers *Indefatigable and Indomitable.* At one point, he witnessed the task force undergo a formation maneuver. He was mesmerized by the shifting of position at over 0.1 C.

But mostly, he endured with his men and counted the minutes until he would be free of his internment.

Roberts' emotions about returning to Gliese were unsettled. The last time he was there, Gallant had commanded this ship.

He moved the *Warrior* to establish a charging base in the asteroid belt. He designated it as outpost Alpha. From there, he scouted the central region of the star system.

The *Warrior* got a glimpse of Titan operations and reported back to the task force.

He established a second outpost on the far side of the asteroid field to observe enemy movements. Roberts reported to Gallant, "Outposts are up and running. The *Warrior* will deliver the Marines to the target asteroid on schedule. Reconnaissance is in progress, with sightings confirmed. You won't believe what we're seeing."

CHAPTER 20

Hawkeye

On D-12, Gallant stepped anxiously into the ready room.

"Atttention!"

"As you were."

All twelve Hawkeye pilots stood in front of their chairs; their eyes followed him as he took the podium in front of them.

Gallant gazed at the faces of seven men and five women, all young and eager, ready to undertake a mission that he hated to send them on.

He smiled and said, "Please be seated. Relax."

He switched on the viewscreen and flipped to the first diagram.

"You've all seen the preliminary search results from the initial Hawkeye and drone sweeps. Our local area is clean. The task force will be able to operate on this edge of the system undisturbed for the next few days."

He wished he was as sure of that as he stated, but for now, that was all the intel they had.

"I have two needs from you today. You know them. First, you must locate the Titan Home Fleet. It was a big relief to find that we weren't at their doorstep when we busted into the system from warp."

There was a loud murmur of agreement.

"We must cast a wide net to find that fleet. We need to know if it can interdict our space wing when they approach Gliese-Beta. And just as importantly, we need to know what we can do to influence their future movements. I've already dispatched a large portion of our drones sunward to scout the path the space wing will follow. Another group has been sent spiraling out from the task force to search for enemy forces."

He showed the flight paths of the drones on the screen.

"We will send eight Hawkeyes to follow sector searches along the best-case locations for the enemy fleet."

He scanned the audience and watched them check the search vectors they might have to execute.

"But that still leaves the most dangerous mission. Four Hawkeyes must go ahead of the space wing's flight path and sweep for passive early warning sensor arrays. These arrays can penetrate our stealth cover at moderate distances."

He took a breath and paused. The most emotional demand

he had to make was coming.

"Every early warning array will have a nearby fighter base for immediate response. So, when you find an array and radio its location back to us, you will also trigger alarms, and a swarm of fighters will be on your tail before you know it. You'll have to turn and run for your lives."

He looked at the pilots. He saw grim determination, not fear.

"The space wing will use the location information to swing around the sensor field, but the Hawkeye pilot will be on his, or her, own. So, I'm asking for volunteers for this."

Every hand but one was raised. Kelsey kept her hand by her side.

Gallant said, "Lieutenant Mitchel, will you select the four pilots from your squadron?"

"Amy, Jerry, Tasha."

"That's three," said Gallant.

"Of course, I will be going as well, Captain. That was obvious," said Kelsey with a slight head bob.

Gallant nodded.

He dispatched the search craft, but he refused to give it more than a casual thought. It was standard operating procedure. Hawkeyes always went out first and charted the safe path to avoid enemy sensors and forces. But he was uneasy about those sectors left uncovered by the search plan.

He studied the search plan with unease. Setting the ships

out had to be done, but he feared it was an effort that threw away the lives of the brave pilots.

At first, Gallant put the thought of Hawkeyes out of his mind, but over the course of the following days, he dwelled more and more on the dangers the Hawkeyes faced—and the fact that Kelsey was in the lead. It wasn't right that he should care so much more about her life. But he did. And it hurt.

Anxiety brought oaths to his lips. He was aware of how senseless the curses were even without uttering them. If only he could obtain the vital information without the cost of the lives of those he sent out without so much as a 'good luck.'

As the Hawkeyes penetrated deep into the system, they discovered several passive sensor fields that were dispersed through the system to detect this kind of attack. When a Hawkeye found an array, it transmitted the location to the *Constellation*. Gallant briefed Ryan, who adjusted the planned starfighter trajectory for the raid. But once a Hawkeye became a highlighted target, it drew enemy fighters to it like bees to a flower. While some Hawkeyes managed to escape, most went silent—never to be heard from again.

CHAPTER 21

Gotcha

On D-8, Task Force 34 skirted along the edge of asteroid field. It trekked to a key transit point where mineral freighters traveled.

There they waited.

Commerce was the lifeblood of the Titan civilization, and the shipping routes between its mining colonies and the inner planets offered an opportunity.

ZXZ! ZXZ! ZXZ!

An unidentified signal came from space.

The sensor operator reported, "Enemy ship, bearing 020 relative, ten light-minutes."

Gallant turned to Fletcher and asked, "What do you make of it?"

"It's got the configuration of a freighter, but it's far from the mining lanes we've mapped out. It's sending a general broadcast with maximum dispersion. It could be a distress call."

Turnbull stepped closer. "It could be a picket ship sending an alert."

Gallant said, "A picket would broadcast a tight high energy beam to a relay station or support vessel."

Fletcher asked, "Why didn't our Hawkeye search find this ship earlier?"

The OOD said, "Its outside our primary search box, Ma'am."

"Even so It's sloppy that it slipped past long-range sensors," said Turnbull.

Gallant couldn't deny that he would have preferred more notice.

"We need to send someone to that ship to shut it up," said Fletcher.

Gallant said, "Make it so."

Fletcher ordered a task force to change course to the Titan ship. When they had the ship on radar, they matched the vessel's velocity and course.

The ship looked like a derelict drifting far from the shipping lanes.

The OOD said, "Something doesn't look right about that ship. Its profile seems strange, and their broadcast keeps repeating, but they are not responding to our messages."

"We don't know how long that distress call has been broadcast. They might have abandoned ship and be far away, in escape pods," said Fletcher.

"It looks too easy," said Turnbull.

"Civilian ships shouldn't be this far from shipping lanes or space facilities."

"They might be pirates or criminals."

"Could be. Or it might be a picket ship to catch attackers like us," repeated Turnbull. "What do you propose?"

"XO, take a boarding party and have a look," said Gallant.

An hour later, Fletcher reached the derelict.

There was no reply from the seemingly dead ship as the shuttle reached her. When they docked, the boarding party entered the main hatch without incident.

They entered the ship, but there was no one to greet them.

Fletcher sent half the party to engineering while she led others to the bridge. They looked for anyone aboard but found none. The team disabled the communication gear to stop the transmission. They went into engineering and sabotaged the engine for good measure.

When they returned to the *Constellation*, Fletcher said, "It looks to me that this ship was abandoned months ago and has been drifting ever since."

"I'm not convinced," said Turnbull. "If it's a picket ship designed to fool an interloper, this would be the kind of ruse I'd employ."

Gallant asked Fletcher, "What kind of communication and sensor gear was onboard?"

"It didn't have sensors capable of reaching as far as our task force even if we weren't under stealth. The communication network looked primitive. Not the sophisticated, powerful technology a picket would use for detecting and broadcasting."

Gallant said, "I think we have found, exactly what this looks like, an abandoned, damaged freighter. I am confident that we haven't been discovered. Our element of surprise is still intact even if the odds just got a little longer."

"You can't be positive about that. I advise you to move the entire timetable up. Launch immediately before the Titan have time to react to our presence," said Turnbull.

Gallant said, "That will put more pressure on the space wing flight time. When you unleash a weapon like Lieutenant Ryan, you must expect the unexpected. He will make choices that you can't predict. Plus, changing the timetable will be impossible for the Marines, not to mention the final rendezvous with the Great Ship."

Gallant spent a few minutes lost in thought. He calculated that the derelict couldn't have automatically reported much, even if it made any report at all. And most likely, the Titan commander receiving such sketchy data would only send a drone out to investigate, and the time required to reach this far would be days. The task force would be far away, and the drone would find nothing.

"I'm willing to bet that we hadn't lost the element of surprise," said Gallant. "We will continue all operations as scheduled. No changes."

Turnbull's face contorted into a mask of anger, but she held her tongue.

CHAPTER 22

Launch

The life cycle of a military operation starts with an embryonic vision and over time develops into a practical reality. Up until that point, it's just a vague dream to the sailors and soldiers involved.

Everything changes on launch day. Once the GO code is given, dreaming and planning are over—a tectonic shift occurs.

Captain Gallant ordered, "Prepare to launch the starfighter wing."

The bridge team tensed as the flight deck exploded in a flurry of last-minute activities, from clearing the launch path to revving engines. Pilots clutched their throttle and fingered safety switches. Flight crews removed chocks while crash teams inched closer, alert to any malfunction.

At 2359 hours, everyone held their breath.

At 0000 hours, Gallant said, "Launch starfighters."

Task Force 34 spacecraft carriers, *Constellation* and *Courageous,* began shooting Vipers into space.

The flight deck was a dangerous place. The short runway gave the crew little margin for error. Each launch required clockwork precision—move starfighters into position on the catapult, raise the blast deflector behind the craft, clear the flight deck, depressurize the hanger. Once the huge doors opened to space, the catapult officer sprung the high-speed piston, slinging the fighter forward while the pilot throttled the engine, which rocketed the fighter to 100 km/s.

Each carrier launched four ships every two minutes. The pace was as treacherous as it was demanding.

Gallant watched it all through the monitors in the flight deck control room. It wasn't hard to be excited and worried at the same time.

Something's wrong.

A problem on the flight deck had stopped launches, and there was a flurry of activity around one of the fighters. Techs were pulling emergency gear out of lockers, and lights were flashing.

Gallant shouted, "Damn. Clear away that gear and reset the launcher."

He was normally a temperate man, but when it came to the

performance and safety of his ship, fear of failure drove him to exasperating hardness.

Here was a case where a rack on the side of a Viper was hung up on scaffolding. The crowded Vipers had caused problems of space and movement. While the upgraded craft had new tanks and external racks, not all the bugs had been worked out.

He sat impatiently until the crew chief announce the problem was cleared. The launches resumed for another ten minutes, then once more problems arose.

Gallant shook his head.

Not an auspicious start.

But it was a start. There was so much more to come.

Gallant sucked in a breath at the incredible sight of his starfighter formation accelerating sunward into the fog of war

Wing Commander Lieutenant Ryan was the first to launch. With a thrill, he took his position at the front of the task force. The starfighter wing of Vipers and Hawkeyes fell into formation behind him.

He nosed out of position to take a firsthand look at the tight formation, feeling good about his team. Everyone was in position.

They had planned and trained for this day for months. Now he scanned his instrument readings and listened to the AI report that the ship was running perfectly.

Ryan hated such long, dull flights. Once he put the ship on

autopilot, the AI ran system checks, navigated, and scanned for contacts and dangerous asteroids. For nine days, he would have nothing to do.

He leaned back and began to daydream about Lorelei, and the last time they fought.

Does she think less of me?

He couldn't forgive himself for drinking before that flight. He had committed an unspeakable act that could have caused harm.

There was no justification.

Since then, he hardly spoke to Lorelei. She didn't return his messages. So, he pretended nothing happened. The transgression was too great, so it had to disappear from his worries. And so, she disappeared as well.

He let out a long, self-pitying sigh.

ALERT! ALERT!

An alarm sounded in his cockpit.

"What's that?!"

He had forgotten to turn off the auto-update feature. His AI was processing routine operations and reached a point where it began a routine update that required a reboot cycle. The AI forced him to take manual control of Lucky 7.

Embarrassed, he radioed, "All pilots check that your auto-update feature is switched off."

They all knew why he was reminding them.

He could imagine their chuckles.

Dusty said over tac1, "Oh, thanks, Wing Commander. I would have been so embarrassed if my AI rebooted in the middle of an operation in hostile territory."

He wasn't the only one. The jeers went on for several minutes. They were so bored that this was their main amusement.

"Glad I could be entertaining for you lugs. Resume radio silence."

He assumed he would spend most of his time sleeping during the journey, but that delusion fled only eight hours into the flight.

A Viper II pilot broke radio silence to report an engine malfunction.

Ryan used his augmented reality connection to the fighter to download data and assess the problem. He examined the readout and ran a series of tests with the help of his AI. What he needed to do came to him as if he had a cheat sheet. All the necessary specifications came bubbling up from his memory into a sparkling cocktail of essential analysis and a straightforward remedy.

He ordered the problem Viper to break formation. He ordered the pilot to conduct a spacewalk to affect a repair under his guidance. It was several hours before the Viper was able to accelerate back to its proper position.

Unfortunately, it was only the first of a series of breakdowns and problems that plagued them throughout the flight.

The extra racks and last-minute upgrades were proving to be unstable.

Workaround became his MO. Every pilot looked to him to manage the fallout of upgrades. He began to wish he had practiced harder and learned more about the changes before they left.

Dark-matter containment tanks were not meant to be controlled for prolonged periods. Leaks occurred on two fighters and a bomber, each requiring a spacewalk fix. They straggled behind, forcing Ryan to debate whether they should return to the *Constellation*.

But what if we lead the Titans back to the task force?

He had to adjust acceleration and orbit to reconcile the downtime of off engines for repair. The AI kept asking him questions he had no answer for.

"What good is an AI if it doesn't know this stuff," he exclaimed.

Three days into the flight, he was getting frantic. The continued delays might upset the D-Day timetable. Yet he had no way to contact the Marines and adjust the schedule.

At last, the bugs seemed to work themselves out. Repairs were completed, ships were running, and the entire starfighter wing was again in tight formation. They received regular target reports from the lead Hawkeye, and their stealth mode held strong.

Once again, Ryan was flying on autopilot. He had completed system checks, and navigation audits with his flight team and was left alone with his thoughts. Tired of waiting for the battle and fed up with all the setbacks, he lapsed into reminiscing. To help him drown out the negative thoughts that flooded in, he switched on a mixtape of his favorite music. He had too many ugly thoughts to turn them loose, especially in the emptiness of space. The memories he tried to block out resurfaced.

He never was able to make lasting relationships with any of his foster parents. Like many orphaned youths, he hadn't had much in the way of parental stability and guidance.

The best memory he had was his emancipation from foster care at the age of 17. Without many supportive adults in his life, he never felt comfortable sharing his inner thoughts and feelings. More recently, that tendency spilled over into emotional relationships, the way it had with Lorelei.

He wished he had brought some alcohol along.

I could use a good stiff drink about now.

The thought brought an instant twinge of remorse. He recalled his last argument with Lorelei and his talk with Gallant. He wanted to repay their trust.

With an effort, he shook off the disturbing memories. Battle was his chance for recognition and approval. The opportunity to earn respect, even love—all the things he never had growing up. Combat seemed easier than examining his childhood. He didn't care if he died in battle. Since he had no family, no connection, death could take nothing from him.

Except, maybe, Lorelei.

CHAPTER 23

Renege

To Gallant's surprise, the Great Ship materialized a few light-minutes ahead of Task Force 34. Almost close enough to render passing honors like ships of old.

This was too early for the rendezvous with the starfighters at point ZED. He had made no provision to speak with the ship before that.

What do the Chameleon want?

Gallant ordered, "Open a channel."

The communication officer said, "The Great Ship asks permission for Ambassador Aurora to come aboard."

Gallant replied in the affirmative and waited for her small craft to arrive, wondering what she could possibly want.

When the Marine guard ushered Aurora into Gallant's stateroom, she appeared calm and unconcerned as she took a seat across from him.

"The situation here is grave," he said.

"It's grave everywhere," was her quiet response.

"A Titan derelict ship was intercepted and disabled. But I assessed that it did not reveal our presence or cause a change in plans."

"I'm sure you are right."

"Then, that is not your concern?"

"No."

"So, you are prepared to carry out your mission as we agreed?"

Aurora sighed, "Alas, we must disappoint you."

"What's the problem?"

"The Great Ship has many demands placed upon her. It's not always easy to fulfill our plans."

"Will you be able to make the rendezvous?"

"I'm afraid not."

Tamping down his anger, Gallant said, "Is there nothing I can do so you can keep your agreement?"

Aurora said, "There is one thing you could do that might allow us to keep our original arrangement."

Gallant waited as tension built in his shoulders.

She said, "Your people must return the Ross star system to the Chameleon."

He frowned. "There are provisions in our treaty that cover how those circumstances would be accommodated once the war is over."

Aurora stood towering over Gallant.

"We cannot wait."

Gallant stood as well, his brows knitted, as the silent organization of his mind spun out of control.

"Why? What has changed? Why do you renege on an agreement that was so hard to establish? Our contract had specific obligations we expect you to meet."

"People can change their minds even after entering a contract."

"But most try to keep their obligations. Negotiating is always a delicate situation, especially when there have been complications or miscommunication over expectations."

Aurora shrugged. "If you do not agree to this amendment, I'm afraid the Great Ship will have to leave this system immediately."

"Many human lives were lost, taking that system from the Titans. I had friends and colleagues die or suffer horrible injuries to drive the enemy out. Our forces are building an infrastructure to prevent the Titans from returning. They are constructing battle stations, missile launchers, and fighter bases. Much of our blood and resources have been poured into the Ross planets."

Gallant spoke with passion and conviction, and he was not prepared for the response he received.

Aurora's face went cold, changing color many times. She said, "Would you like me to provide you with a list of the Chameleon people who were born on those planets? Who were murdered on those planets by the Titan? Would you care to match the lives of our soldiers who were exterminated when the Titan dropped nuclear bombs on the planets?"

She looked at him questioningly. "No, gifted one?" using the term of endearment, almost like a weapon.

"I can appreciate your pain, but I am disappointed that you will not honor and respect our treaty. In any event, I do not have the authority to renegotiate our agreement."

"You were a lead member of Earth's negotiating delegation. You met with the Lord Protector. We recognize you as speaking for your government, and we will accept your commitment as binding in our legal system. The courts can thrash out a final determination later, but it all starts with your agreement now. Otherwise, we will not take part in the recovery of your fighters."

Gallant thought about Steward's Marines. They were at this very moment landing on the Titan asteroid fighter base. And he thought about Ryan's space wing nearing Gliese-Beta. He was faced with a heartbreaking decision to sacrifice his starfighters or give up the hard-fought-for position at Ross.

He felt as if an unfair burden had been added on top of all that he already carried.

He tried to calculate the outcome of abandoning the Ross system, but there was no prescription that could foretell the side-effects of such an event.

Dismayed, he softly said, "We will agree to turn the Ross

system over to the Chameleon but through a phased withdrawal. As Chameleon forces occupy defensive positions, our forces will withdraw."

"Thank you, gifted one," she said with a smile. She glowed with approval. She raised her hand to touch him, but he moved back out of reach.

Gallant realized the truth about her powers and intentions. Neither of which he admired. He felt exhausted by the constant pressure she exerted on his mind.

He said, "You should leave now. I expect you have preparations to make to reach point ZED."

Turnbull? What am I going to tell Turnbull?

That night, Gallant tossed and turned, unable to find sleep. Doubts and fears crowded his mind, unwilling to leave, and slumber could not find its way in.

CHAPTER 24

Gung Ho

While Gallant was meeting with Aurora, the *Warrior* and *Invidia* approached the Titan fighter base from the dark side of the asteroid. They remained under cloak, side by side, a thousand kilometers over the asteroid's surface.

There were only three days left before D-day.

The bridge crew was tense, ready to become visible, and maneuver the ship close to the asteroid to minimize the Cobras' flight time.

"Drop cloak," ordered Roberts. "Prepare to launch Cobras."

A high-pitched whistle sounded over the ship's intercom.

"Attention all hands. Approaching drop zone."

The operations chief opened the *Warrior's* hangar doors.

The Cobra pilots were switching power settings.

"Marines hook-up."

The Marines clipped themselves to the tether, hoping the cable was strong enough to keep them from drifting away.

The Cobras flew out of the hangar bay with tethers deployed like tails.

Aboard the *Invidia*, the same procedure was taking place.

The two ships approached their target.

Roberts ordered, "Drop cloak."

The helmsman reported, "Stealth is de-energized."

Roberts ordered, "Open hangar doors. Deploy Cobras."

When the first Cobra flew off the deck, the Marines looked like a string of beads dangling behind on the tether.

Sonny gave a "Yahoo!"

McCauley barked, "Silence."

When all the Cobra were gone, Roberts ordered, "Maximum stealth."

The two ships disappeared back into the anonymous void of space.

The Cobras flew two kilometers over the ground. Each space-jet trailed a one-hundred-meter cable with a platoon of Marines attached. Their target was a mountainous area filled with ravines and gully that would afford cover.

"Sergeant, ready?" asked the pilot.

"Ready."

"Go,"

McCauley signaled the platoon, and they released their

hooks and ignited their jetpacks. Falling to the surface with their jetpacks was now second nature to them. They controlled the jets by tilting the handgrips to set the vectors of the engine thrust; twisting left hand moved two nozzle skirts for yaw; twisting the right hand counterclockwise increased the throttle.

They landed together in a coordinated formation and spread out into a defensive perimeter to secure the landing zone. Next, they set about expanding the lodgment.

The rocky terrain was the color of pain—black and blue—as Sonny learned when he lost his balance and landed hard.

McCauley asked, "Anyone hurt?"

Sonny sprang to his feet. "All good here."

"Deploy scout drones," said Steward.

A few minutes later, he asked, "Do you see anything?"

"Looks clear out to 10 kilometers," said McCauley.

Steward hesitated a moment, but decisions had to be made.

"Battalion, forward!" ordered Steward leading the vanguard.

The Marines had 500 kilos of supplies in backpacks for the 200-kilometer trek to reach their attack positions. The expected one-sixth Earth-normal gravity was helpful. The sandy, rocky surface produced bumps and bruises they had become familiar with on the moon.

Here was where the hard training on the moon paid off. The Marines endured the hundreds of kilometers clandestine march through enemy territory. They were ready and willing.

During the day's trek across the barren landscape, they moved in rhythm with bouncy steps. Tension mounted as they maintained cover. It was difficult to move across the asteroid. Concealed within the nooks and crannies of the rock-strewn terrain, they were like a caterpillar crawling toward a picnic blanket. The jagged ridges and lofty volcanic fumes were scattered in front of them. So far, they went unnoticed. They knew the coming battle on land and in space would be costly in both soldiers and sailors, but they tempered their anxiety with the thought of purpose.

Scouts and drones were well ahead of the main body. They reported no indication that they were discovered by the Titans.

Steward received drone reports of Titan troop movements on the asteroid to and from barracks. He worried which were routine and which might show that he was discovered. He identified security patrols and laid out a trap to ambush them at the right moment if necessary.

On D-2, Sergeant McCauley reported, "All companies are moving in good order."

Steward was relieved that the updated drone photos of the actual target were like the mock facilities they trained on.

"Good. I'll lead Able company," said Steward. "Keep up the pace. I'll send instructions as we continue."

The sergeant said, "You should stay with the main body."

"The best place for me is at the forefront," said Steward,

"Keep the men together. Don't let anyone fall behind."

In the darkness, there were scrambling footsteps behind them. The companies were straggling with occasional swearing as someone fell.

Steward set off. His heart pounded as his lungs strained to inhale. Sweat gushed from every pore in his body. His legs cramped with each step as his feet sank into the grainy terrain.

His eyes took time to adjust to the dim light as they swept the distance. There were only round hills ahead.

He had hoped to reach one of the targeted areas at the edge of the mountain range.

I may have miscalculated, he thought.

Shifting his backpack to his other shoulder, he faced east and plodded forward. The hot, dry recycled air buffeted his irritated skin. He walked only a few kilometers before he had to stop and take a drink. The process repeated itself as his muscles continued to cramp.

His parched throat cried for water, but he rationed what remained. The growl from his stomach, he ignored as well. As he glanced behind him, the tiny craters his steps left were disappearing under the shifting sand.

Two days of travel through the rocks had not seemed too demanding when he planned the mission. Now he was hitting a wall.

He traveled while licking his lips and swallowing to relieve his dehydrated throat. It was a grueling struggle, but when he reached the crest of a mountain ridge, he had a clear view eastward. He remained alert for any sign of the enemy, but it remained a barren asteroid.

It must have been his obsession with looking in the distance that left him vulnerable to his closest surroundings, and he tripped.

His body felt the impact, and he took a few minutes to rest.

On D-1, the Marines reached a long ridge they could follow. It was a long hard climb up the canyons, hard ground soon became loose rocks, and then small boulders became obstructions. Men stomped along the trail with their weapons and equipment.

Steward surveyed the landscape. "We're on the crest. You can see a gully and an outcrop."

"About twenty kilometers to target?" asked McCauley.

"Possibly less."

"Let's get closer and see how the ridgeline lays out."

He examined his AR map to reconcile its images with what his eyes were seeing.

"There's a useful path with no obstructions. Sergeant, you guide the main body to this point. I'm going onward."

"Everyone's ready for action."

It was time for the four companies of Marines to separate and approach their individual targets. Companies Able and Baker would hit the fighter command center and its backup. The other two companies would destroy the individual fighters on the base.

They moved off in diverging trails that were a painful sight.

If one failed, they all failed. They watched each unit receding, and with that, the tension increased, and the sense of security diminished. They maneuvered closer to their target.

"Okay," he said to McCauley, "I'll go with Abel company for the final push. You set the fire watch."

After an hour, he brought Able company to the point where they could take a break. It was an anxious moment as they approached the dominating physical feature of the ridge peak. Though none had slept, and they had marched a long hard distance, they were in good spirits.

Steward sat with his men getting ready for final preparations.

He said, "There are guards on the ridge behind a fence. They have a defensive position with a trench followed by a low barricade."

"Not what we were expecting," said the sergeant with a frown.

Steward asked, "What's your assessment?"

"The above-ground defenses are stronger than we thought, but its what's inside that bunker waiting for us that troubles me?"

Steward said, "Once we can take the outer position, those inside don't have a chance."

He studied the map. "Will our men be fast enough?"

McCauley nodded.

The ridge barricade fence was the key defensive above ground. Beneath the bunker was the tunnel system that extended throughout the mountain range. Once they breached that strong point, there was no stopping them.

From Steward's study of the tunnel network, the underground bunker was built to withstand nuclear bombs. But it was not designed to resist a direct ground assault.

He hammered home that, "Surprise is everything."

Several guards were patrolling, but they failed to discover the Marines.

Steward gave his final orders, and the men prepared for their assault. They remained hidden in a gully a hundred meters from the fence while the final seconds ticked away.

CHAPTER 25

What If

The communications officer broke the tense silence on the bridge of the *Constellation*. "Captain, we're receiving a mayday from a Hawkeye."

After a week, eight Hawkeye were due to return to the *Constellation*. So far, only one had, and there was only one more unaccounted for.

Gallant stared at the display. "Which one?" he asked, his voice breaking.

Kelsey?

"Unclear, sir. The ship was on its way back from the penetration mission and ran into a Titan patrol. It ... it's stopped transmitting now, but it reported significant damage from enemy fire. We'll have to wait until it lands to learn more."

Gallant's fingers dug into the armrests.

"How long until recovery?"

"At least an hour, sir. The craft is flying erratically."

He was furious with himself for sending Kelsey on such a hazardous mission. He would never forgive himself if she was taken from him.

Impatiently, he rose and said, "I'll be on the flight deck if you need me,"

He spent the interminable wait pacing around the flight deck control room, obsessing over Kelsey. The first time they met on the *Repulse,* their partnership as copilots in the Eagle in combat against the Titans, the moment after their battle in the asteroids when he thought she wouldn't survive her wounds. The same anxiety now tore at his gut.

He watched the radar screen tracing the Hawkeye's erratic flight. As the ship approached the landing bay, he winced at an alarm signaling divergent trajectory. Even as the controller barked adjustment orders to the pilot, the landing crew had no idea whether the craft's communication system could receive them.

In its final approach, the Hawkeye veered first to port then to starboard, only to finish too high. Fortunately, the craft careened straight into the protective crash net, which kept it from slamming into the ship's hull.

The chamber had barely pressurized before Gallant ran to the ship. When the hatch flipped open, the stench of a scorched flight suit almost overwhelmed him.

He coughed and waved his arms to disperse the smoke, trying to see the pilot. It took several agonizing seconds for the air to clear.

Then he gasped with relief. "Kelsey? Kelsey, are you all right?"

"Captain. Yes. I think so. At least, nothing serious."

He couldn't stop himself from crushing her in a hug. "I'm so glad you're okay. I was so worried!"

"I'm okay, Henry, really. I'm all right."

She looked uncertainly at him, puzzled at his attention. "After all the dead fighter pilots and Marines, after all the destruction you've seen, you came down to the flight deck to wait for one errant Hawkeye pilot?"

He stared at her, unable to respond.

"Why, Henry?"

Nonplused, Gallant couldn't answer. Finally, after a minute, he said, "Get yourself cleaned up. And when you've had a chance to unwind, please see me in my cabin."

An hour later, Kelsey joined Gallant in his cabin off the bridge.

"You were about to tell me why you were so upset, Captain."

"Kelsey, we share a history, a bond that means a lot to me."

"A bond? A history?"

"Remember when we first met as Midshipmen?"

"Of course."

"What did you think of me then?"

She broke into a broad smile. "You were very awkward . . . and very eager."

"And later . . . when we started dating?"

She said nothing but tilted her head to one side, lost in thought.

"Did you ever think we would be . . .?"

"No," she interrupted, just shaking her head. "No, I was already dating Anton when you asked me out."

"But you went with me. I thought . . .."

"You were never really right for me."

He put his hand in his pocket and fingered a tiny memory disc. He had diligently rid himself of all aspects of their past relationship—all but this one memento—a single song that Kelsey sang in a tavern on Jupiter station when they were midshipman. Now, as he reviewed his past, he saw the deep gulf he had left between his desires and his choices.

"Not right? How do you mean?" he couldn't disguise the hurt in his voice.

She sighed. "You were always too cerebral . . . and too hesitant. I'm sorry, but I never loved you, not that way. I always thought highly of you, and I cherish our friendship, but it was never more than that."

"Then you never considered, what if you had chosen me instead of Anton."

She shrugged. "Anton was bold, decisive. Not to mention incredibly handsome." She seemed to sink in the memory. "With his perfect profile, blond hair, and cat-like agility, he reminded me of a Viking."

She added with a little laugh. "And his blue eyes were awfully hard to resist."

Gallant felt flushed with envy. He tried to deal with the stifled memories, packed with regret.

She asked, "How well did you know Anton while you were on the *Repulse*?"

"He wasn't very open. I hardly knew more than a thimbleful."

"Typical. He put up barriers. His rich father dominated him and drove him to strive for perfection. I met Gerome Neumann early in my relationship with Anton. He liked me and encouraged his son to pursue me. I was flattered beyond measure."

Gallant thought back to the first moment he met Anton in the midshipmen's quarters aboard the *Repulse*. The first words out of Anton's mouth had been to ask what Gallant's genetic quotient was. He knew from then on that they would never be friends. Anton's measuring stick for friendship was on a different scale than his. As the genetically engineered perfectionist, Anton had nothing but scorn for Gallant, the Natural—one without any status or worth.

Anton's inscrutable face and acerbic wit made him difficult to fathom. Nevertheless, he embodied the finest attributes of a fighter pilot. Gallant was always impressed with Anton's outstanding performance and wanted to emulate him.

He said, "So, you were confronted by this rich, brilliant, handsome man and you...?"

"I never told you how he proposed," she smiled. "He took me out in his fighter and treated me to every hair-raising maneuver ever invented. Then he plunged the fighter into a steep dive straight toward the planet. He said if I didn't accept his marriage proposal right then, he would smash the ship into the Earth. We would both die in a fiery crash and become a modern-day Romeo and Juliet."

Gallant felt the bitter taste of jealousy in his mouth.

"To this day, I still wonder if he would have gone through with it," she said, her eyes distant. "He always had the ability to keep you on a razor's edge. He swept me off my feet, and I said yes... as it turned out, maybe too quickly for both of us. I was starry-eyed and deliriously happy for a few moments. I believe his proposal was sincere, but I soon realized that he was a spoiled rich kid who was more interested in the conquest than the commitment. His attention was already wandering before our honeymoon was over."

"Do you regret marrying him?"

She sighed. "Not at first. As I said, he literally took my breath away. But despite his blazing passion, all too soon, I realized how willful, egotistical, and selfish he was. Our love never sang in harmony. So, yes. I came to have regrets. In retrospect, he wasn't right for me."

He asked again, "What if...?"

"No." She shook her head. "You weren't right for me either, Henry. I hope I do find the right person someday. But you and I would have made a hopeless wreck of a marriage."

These were not the words he wanted to hear. He longed to hear that she regretted not choosing him—that they would have shared a wonderful life together.

Seeing his dismay, she said, "You can't reshuffle the deck and deal again. Those cards have been played. You have to live in the here and now."

Gallant relived the same gut-wrenching emotional loss he had experienced when Kelsey had turned him down years before.

After a little while, he did not regret learning the circumstances of his vain frustrations. But he realized the foolish waste of further intrigue.

"Don't be upset." She shook her head. "In your heart, you know you've found the right woman, even if you're too blind to appreciate her. Alaina is the perfect match for you. Any fool can see that. She knows it."

Kelsey touched his cheek. "And you should too."

CHAPTER 26

Thunder and Lightning

D-Day was an hour away.

Lieutenant Rob Ryan's starfighters approached the second planet in the Gliese star system, hoping their odd trajectory would do the trick. They flew out of the sun, high above the star's ecliptic plane, using the Chameleon stealth enhancements.

At 00:00, the starfighters thundered high over the clear sky of Gliese-Beta.

Ryan broadcast, "Thunder! Thunder! Thunder!"

The signal that the starfighters had achieved total surprise.

To the Titans, it was a shock. Their early warning system had failed. Only when the starfighters were poised to launch, did the Titans radars become aware of the danger.

For the pilots, who left the *Constellation* and *Courageous* days earlier, the mission had become a reality. The predictions during the mission readiness briefing no longer matter. Things now got complicated as the pilots began reacting to their cunning enemy.

Ryan thought, *How cunning?*

He faced planetary defenses of twenty-four battle stations, one hundred missile bases, and 484 fighters.

The squadrons worked together to coordinate their actions, under the guidance of Ryan's mental picture of the battlespace. He felt good. He was perfectly clear. He knew what to do and how to do it.

The starfighters were several million kilometers from the planet when Ryan ordered, "Prepare for formation retro."

A second later, he ordered, "Execute!"

Each starfighter applied its gyros to flip the ship on its axis 180 degrees. The ship's tails were now facing the planet as they applied maximum acceleration—effectively applying the 'brakes' to the space wing.

As the ships decelerated from 0.1 C to a mere hundred kilometers per second, Ryan ordered, "Starfighters, standby to break into separate attack flights."

A moment later, he ordered, "Break!"

The split was well executed.

Ryan said, "Godspeed."

The many hours of precision flying were paying off. The ninety-six bombers broke into eight distinct flights seeking eight different targets. The sixty-six fighters broke into eight separate protection details. A lone Hawkeye flew high above to assess the damage and any Titan counterattack.

The United Planets' flights broke up into their mission objectives and followed GPS coordinates to their targets. They flew over a jagged course to confuse radars and throw off intercepting fighters.

The eight flights sped on their separate paths. Even after slowing down, they were traveling so fast that the AI had difficulty calculating target locations. Each mission group followed an irregular path to target to deceive the enemy about their destination.

As the flights separated, Ryan and his eight Vipers focused their attention on Flight 1's twelve bombers led by Lorelei. They were his primary focus now. All his attention was directed at their safety. He still had an AI trace of the other flights, but his tactical requirements were now centered on Lorelei's bombers and their target, the Titan capital city.

"Flight 1, stay tight," urged Ryan as he led his fighters into action against the first group of Phantoms.

Glenn Holman peeled to port and took his position behind Ryan's right wing.

It was only a couple of minutes until Lorelei's flight steadied on attack trajectory.

Only now were the Titan planetary warning sirens screeching.

EEEEEEERRRR!!

Ryan's display showed red flares on the planet's surface.

"Incoming missiles," warned Ryan.

A few seconds later, his AI reported, "Enemy fighters launched from four separate locations. The nearest is directly ahead."

Ryan saw the Titan fighters rising from the surface. They were fighting the planet's gravity, struggling to reach combat speed.

That'll take several minutes.

In the meantime, Flight 1 had business to conduct.

Lorelei's Viper was in the lead of the first flight of bombers, targeting the capital city. It was lonely but somehow satisfying to be so disconnected from the rest of the universe. Yet she knew that at any moment she could be surrounded by enemies. Ryan's flight of fighters was supposed to cover her, but he was gone, caught up in a dogfight with Titan fighters.

Lorelei's flight met no initial resistance. They were getting ready to launch their first set of missiles from the external racks. Then the city's bristling defense lit up the sky. Plasma guns and missiles raced skyward at her flight. So many things happened at once that there was no way to keep track. A momentary impulse of fear vanished as she twisted her ship away from a sky filled with tracers.

One bomber was lost immediately. More followed in quick succession.

She swooped into a lower orbit to release incendiary missiles at the military targets. Her flight followed suit. She aimed her ship's nose at the enemy and charged ahead.

Lorelei said, "Stay on course. Keep your weapons on target!"

A moment later. "Missiles away!"

The NON-nuclear weapons destroyed military fortifications and production sites. The explosions were a satisfying sight even from a height of 1000 kilometers. The actual damage inflicted on the city was not great, but the psychological impact on the Titan people was calculated to be alarming. No enemy had ever reached their home star, let alone their capital city. The Titans would be kept guessing if the next time the explosives would be nuclear.

Phantoms rose from the planet, and for a moment, it looked like some would catch the bombers, but then two Vipers broke up the attack.

As the battle over the planet ebbed and flowed, the growing number of Titan fighters were having an impact. The battle was only minutes old, but many had died already.

A touch of fear registered in the back of Lorelei's mind. Was it possible that she doubted herself? No. She had something to prove. She took in a deep breath and pointed her ship at the enemy city.

Lorelei ordered, "Clear racks!"

She released the last load of missiles on the target. The remaining missiles and bombs from flight-1 followed. The entire attack was conducted at incredible speed made possible by AI targeting.

Each of the bomber flight commanders reported, "Mission accomplished."

Lorelei broadcast, "Lightning! Lightning! Lightning!"

That was the signal that all targets were hit.

The bombers had expended all their armament. It was time to go home.

In a brisk voice, she said, "Break contact. Change course to match the rendezvous trajectory. Remember, you have limited fuel and environmental capabilities. Good luck!"

She set the flight on their escape course several thousand kilometers from the planet.

Once the surprise was achieved, the bombing was the easy part of the mission. The enemy wasn't ready to respond until that moment. But now the over four hundred Phantoms of the planet were rising into space like angry bees protecting their violated hive.

Over tac 1, she reported, "I have three fighters on my tail. I need help."

As the Titan ships closed in on her, she ejected her external rack and fuel tanks. She hoped it would take only a few minutes for her support fighters to reach her, so she maneuvered to stay alive until then.

"AI, what are the enemy's converging trajectories?"

The Viper's video console displayed color-coded lines and escape avenues. She welcomed the information as she maneuvered to minimize her visibility. But even with the AI data, she still needed to account for the enemy pilot's skill. She maneuvered to avoid enemy fire and aimed her plasma and laser weapons to hit where the enemy would feel it.

She breathed a sigh of relief when the three fighters were intercepted by Ryan and his wingman.

His ship swung into their path, and he fired a hail of destruction. One Titan was destroyed immediately. A second followed. Then Holman got the third.

Lorelei said, "Thanks, Lucky."

As she straightened her course, more enemy fighters came in. The first exchange of fire scored no hits on either side. They were moving so fast that the fighters swept by without a hit.

She looked for help, but Ryan and Holman were surrounded and fighting for their lives.

Once again, Lorelei found herself on her own. As she turned to port, she saw a Titan turn to chase her.

She launched a missile at point-blank range that found its target. The ship exploded, but not before its lasers had splashed against her hull.

"Warning. Power failure," reported the AI.

She was light-headed, and only the appearance of more fighters brought her back to reality. She did the only thing she could think of—she switched to backup power and accelerated away.

Immediately, the aliens fired missiles after her.

She released decoys and fired two antimissiles. The AMM-5 Mongooses flushed from their racks. As the Titan missiles raced toward her, she felt her AI system working to home in on the targets.

One missile exploded.

Her ship twisted and leaped in response to her thoughts.

Then the other missile exploded behind her.

Her survival instincts took over, and an escape path opened as she followed the curved path out of the line of fire.

Lorelei's head throbbed, and her muscles ached from tension. But before the last enemy fighter could shoot, she launched her missile.

The missile exploded, and the enemy was gone.

After a frightful few minutes, she had control and leveled off.

With effort, she maneuvered away.

The next few minutes were a blur as she operated more on instinct than reason.

She wrenched the Viper into a bone-crushing turn and fired her last missile. The shock wave as the explosion filled her viewscreen. She cursed and twisted free of the flurry of Titan fighters.

Too close.

Then she heard, Ryan yell, "Incoming missile!"

Out of the corner of her eye, she saw Ryan fire antimissiles. His aim was good.

The missile exploded behind her.

Turning her gaze back to her escape route, Lorelei said, "I'm getting out of here while I can."

Propelling the Viper upward in a tight spiral away from the attacking ships, she concentrated on her escape path. With thrusters at maximum, the ship's engines strained to accelerate even as she fled.

After several more minutes, she fell in with a withdrawing group of starfighters, heading toward point ZED.

Only a small force of enemy fighters remained circling above Gliese-Beta. Many hundreds of Phantoms were pursuing the retreating starfighters.

She turned her attention to escape. They had to stay ahead of the pursuing Phantoms, accelerating to fight the planet's gravitational pull.

Lorelei patted her control panel and muttered, "Keep it together, baby. Those guys look mad. And there are a lot of them."

CHAPTER 27

Over the Top

On D-Day 00:00, Steward ordered the 1st Marine Raider Battalion to attack. The four individual companies set their action plans in motion. They had reached the critical moment upon which everything depended.

Steward was with Able company in a position to begin an assault on the Titan Fighter Command Center. Bravo company moved in on the nearby backup facility. Companies Charlie and Delta began to infiltrate the fighter base hangars and launch facilities.

He examined the enemy's guard posts along the perimeter of the FCCC. Able company intended to penetrate the perimeter and break into the underground bunker. He would use machine guns and mortars only if necessary.

Steward nudged Captain Arthur with his elbow.

"Forward," ordered Arthur over tac 1, getting Able company moving.

From behind a rock formation at the edge of the perimeter, Arthur ordered, "First squad, take position at the north fence."

The Marines crept forward. This was all choreographed according to their past training exercises.

Master Sergeant McCauley knew what he had to do when the opportunity presented itself. Until then, he waited.

A Titan drone flew a kilometer off to the south. Steward launched one of his drones that homed in on the sentry drone and shot it down. The UP drone then swooped down and released a low level targeted EMP pulse near a sensor power panel, disabling it. The blinking sensor lights on the electrified fence went out.

Steward stood up and scrambled to the tripwire on the north side. He could just make out a sentry passing nearby, but McCauley had already stepped from the shadows and fired a pencil-tight laser beam that sliced through the Titan's neck.

The first squad went through the fence and passed the fallen guard in an instant.

There was no sign of alarm from within the facility.

"All clear," said McCauley.

Steward, rifle in hand, moved forward over the craggy surface, arriving at the edge of the main building. First squad gathered around him.

From the fence line, Arthur ordered, "Second squad take

your position."

Steward could barely make out the figures as they approached the east side of the building. McCauley had vanished once more.

A few minutes later, a second sentry's body dropped to the ground. The second squad was through the fence at the east wall.

This was all orderly and yet unreal as if they were performing a practice exercise back on the moon.

Steward nodded once more, and Arthur ordered the third squad to proceed to the west wall, which they did as efficiently as their predecessors.

A roving sentry appeared and looked as if he was wondering where the other guards were. But before he could investigate, McCauley stood up in front of him. The guard was so surprised he didn't move until a laser beam passed through his throat.

Arthur ordered, "Attach ordinance."

In tandem, the three squads placed plastic explosives on the wall in the shape of a circular door.

Steward heard, "Ready," three times, and moved the men back to the fence line.

When everything was prepared, Arthur touched Steward's arm, and Steward gave him a nod.

Arthur said, "Fire in the hole!"

The three simultaneous explosions sent bright light and debris flying across the area. The explosions also blew three holes in the bunker. Confused shouts from within confirmed the surprise of the attack.

"Make entry," ordered Steward.

The Marines secured the perimeter, and three squads entered the newly created doors while the rest of the company moved up behind them.

Steward entered the north face of the facility with the first squad. The ground was littered with broken pieces from the wall. He moved forward to the first checkpoint, which was an intersection of corridors. His eyewear showed thermal imaging, and the AI augmented-reality feed listed targets as they occurred.

Titan guards began to emerge, one at a time, from various doors, but they were quickly shot by the Marines.

The Marines moved methodically through the passages in a staggered formation, leading every turn with a rifle barrel. With practiced ease, they maintained an interlocked fire zone ahead of them. Headlamps flickered down the corridors and flashed into a room as they passed.

"Clear," called the point Marine.

They meticulously pointed their guns forward and let their headlamps shine on the corridor ahead. Moving past each door and intersection, they announced, "Clear."

Steward prodded, "Go. Go."

At the next intersecting corridor, a Marine said, "Clear."

But a moment later, "Contact. Hot. Target at one o'clock."

The next moment, a half-dozen guns fired at the enemy target.

Pfft! Pfft! Pfft!
Pfft! Pfft! Pfft!

He was eliminated.

Once again, the Marines' training paid dividends.

Surprised out of their sleep, the Titans stumbled around in the half-light, unsure of what was happening and how to respond. At every encounter, the Marines were a step ahead. They knew the layout of the facility, the guard points, the intersections where the enemy could interdict them, and they moved confidently and without hesitation. Steward and his men shot the Titan soldiers as fast as they appeared in the doorways.

Steward had been in many battles. At some point, they had all deteriorated into chaos. But so far, this operation into the fighter control center was picture-perfect. It was as if they were actors in a movie where the script was written by the Marines.

One after another, the corridors and rooms were cleared, and the Titans were cut down before they could group and form a unified defense.

"Halt!" yelled Steward.

They had reached the vaulted door of the main control room.

He ordered, "Attach ordinance,"

Once more, the three squads outlined doors against the inner vault chamber using plastic explosives. A moment later, simultaneous eruptions opened a path into the inner sanctum.

He said, "Sweep the building and set charges at every computer station and junction box."

"Do you see anything outside?" he asked McCauley.

He laughed, "They're still putting on their booties."

"Okay, but as soon as demolition is done, I want a defensive perimeter set up to fend off any counterattack."

"Aye aye, sir."

Steward joined Arthur and the demolition team. The beams of light from his headlamp shone on one charge being set. He was so mesmerized by the process that he lost track of the rest of the activities going on around him.

He could see the control center with hundreds of computer desks. The huge room was in chaos as Titan technicians were scrambling to escape only to find there was no path to safety. The Marines shot every one of them.

Steward turned around as the rest of the company reached the control center.

When the charges were detonated, the uncanny blue methane flame of escaping gases combined with the flammable building materials was creating a scene from hell.

It brought him back to the present.

"Let it burn," he said.

This was the high point of the attack. They had eliminated most of the guards within the building, but Steward expected a nearby guard barracks was now coming alive and would soon send in reinforcements.

Five minutes later, the Titans made a disorganized assault,

but by then it was too late. The Titan's primary Fighter Command & Control Center was in ashes.

The Titan's showed determination and attempted to drive the Marines back, but the Marines held their ground. Grenades and heavy weapon fire slowed the enemy's progress.

When they were ready, Steward ordered the Marines to withdraw from the shattered building.

They did so in good order.

Steward never thought he would be leading a raider battalion, much less that he would be the tip of the spear assaulting a critical Titan target in their home star system. He was starring in a role that might provide a legitimate chance to win the war. Did Marine command see this coming? He hadn't had great appraisal reviews during his first few years, and he wasn't convinced he had earned the right to be here. Nevertheless, here he was.

Able company assembled on the ridge outside the FCCC.

Steward asked, "McCauley, what's the headcount?"

"No KIA. Three wounded but ambulatory."

"That's unbelievable."

"Practice makes perfect," grinned the sergeant.

"Get the men moving back to the rendezvous point."

The attack on this target had been a cakewalk. It was like hitting all green lights while driving through the center of the city.

As the sergeant hurried the troops, he opened the general command channel to contact the other companies and get their reports.

"Bravo company has destroyed the backup FCCC as neatly as Able," reported McCauley. "Delta company attached explosives to many of the base's fighters and destroyed over one hundred fighters in their hangars. They also set fire to the surrounding area before withdrawing."

Then came the bad news.

McCauley said, "However, Charlie company is pinned dawn and hasn't destroyed their target, sir."

Steward studied the AR terrain chart with misgivings. There just weren't enough Marines.

"McCauley get the men moving double-quick. Able company will go to the aid of Charlie company. Bravo and Delta will go set up a perimeter to cover our withdrawal."

Charlie company was over ten kilometers away and in a desperate fight.

The operation had a bad start when a series of ravines were found to be booby-trapped. Casualties were heavy. The ground was crumpled with broken rocks, which slowed down the exhausted men. But the hours of grinding marching during training now paid off. Able company was on the move.

"Come on! Hustle!" Steward kept up a steady encouraging chatter over tac 1 as he led the way as fast as he could over the broken ground.

Once they reached the perimeter of the fighter base, they began laying down a strong fire. Steward ordered the company to crawl forward. When they were close, he yelled, "Fire!"

"McCauley, take the first platoon and set up a covering fire team along those rocks,"

Steward ordered the company to charge and break through the Titan ring to relieve Charlie company. He wanted to strike the enemy position in a single wave, but it was a ragged disorganized line when it reached the enemy. The men were out of breath. They were fumbling, falling, and climbing back up.

The odds were against him, but Steward had often been surprised when math failed to deliver on expectations. He gulped down his anxiety as the realization came that he was running out of options. The thought sent shivers over his spine. He had plenty of time to reconsider, but convention would not allow it. He told himself that fate would dictate his course of action. That conclusion helped him to shrug off further concern.

Unfortunately, Able company had run directly into the teeth of the Titan strength. The unexpected exchange had cost forty casualties. He thrust his gun forward, aimed, and fired. With all the bravado he could muster, he thrust himself forward, firing and killing the aliens in succession. He shook with excitement, even though the well-trained part of him responded sensibly by reminding him to remain calm.

He ordered, "Bring up the machine guns."

Dat-dat-dat-dat-dat-dat-dat-dat-dat-dat!

The spray of machine-gun fire added to the Marines firepower.

For the next hour, the Marines moved over the torturous ground one foot at a time. To overcome the impasse, Steward threw in his reserve platoon.

They ran forward.

Gunfire exploded in a thundering blast. It was like a scene from an inferno, chaos and havoc descended.

Titan reinforcements were pouring in over the hills surrounding the fighter base.

Steward shouted over the mic, "Gather along the ridge!"

Nearly a hundred Phantoms remained operational on the base, but he no longer had the capacity to destroy them on the ground.

He thought, *I'll be lucky if I can get the remnants of Able and Charlie companies back to the rally point.*

In the center of Charlie company, her captain and a few others were struggling to break out of their encirclement. Beyond them were the bodies of many dead Marines.

He called to Steward, "I need covering fire. I need covering fire."

Steward ordered Able company, "Covering Fire! Covering Fire!"

The rifles opened up.

Pfft! Pfft! Pfft!

Followed by the machine guns.

Dat-dat-dat-dat-dat-dat-dat-dat-dat-dat!

CHAPTER 28

Decoy

While Steward and his Marines were detonating their charges at the Titan FCCC, the Constellation crept sunward from the fringes of the star system. Titan civilian traffic in the area looked normal. Gallant wondered about the starfighters and Marines—their battle had begun, but signs of war had not yet reached him. Perhaps the situation wasn't as dire as he feared.

The last few days had passed in a blur—from the moment he launched the strike force through the interminable waiting. The atmosphere aboard the ship was one of growing impatience. The crew wanted to get on with their mission.

He said, "OOD, open the data network in the flag conference room, gather the senior commanding officers for a video conference. And ask the XO and Captain Turnbull to attend."

"Aye aye, sir."

Gallant went to the video conference room and took his place at the podium—the room was completely empty without table or chairs.

A Marine stood at attention at the door as Fletcher and Turnbull entered and stood next to Gallant. Turnbull made an entry into a journal she was keeping. She let Gallant know his performance would be reviewed.

The OOD opened a channel and said, "Commodore, the senior commanding officers are present on-line."

Gallant looked around the room at the full-size three-dimensional holographic images of each officer. He saw eager, expectant faces.

There was Captain Ramsey of the *Indomitable*. He had long, sable hair, high cheekbones, and round black eyes. He wore one of his famous looks, the kind that seemed capable of eating through the titanium of a ship's hull. He was a powerful and commanding figure.

Captain Hernandez of the *Invincible* was next. A muscular, lanky man with eyes that gleamed and blinked, he had a broad face with a full mustache. He was professional in all things.

When Gallant glanced across the table at Captain Jackson of the *Courageous*. She was a lean, dark-skinned, middle-aged woman with a withering stare that made her hard features look stronger.

The senior officers seemed eager to hear from their commander what the next step in the operation was and how they would carry it out.

He knew how they felt. It was all anticipation and emptiness, everything associated with waiting that tore at the gut of a warrior.

The tension of the officers was clear. The last few days had passed in a whirl; from the moment they launched the starfighters through the long period of waiting. The atmosphere aboard the ships was one of growing impatience to 'get on with it.'

He gave Fletcher a searching look. "Commander Fletcher, please give us a status report on Operation Damocles."

The officers looked anxious for news.

She began, "We have received a report from the *Warrior* that the insertion of the Marine Battalion was successfully completed. Major Steward's raiders were well underway toward their objectives in the last report. They have not been detected and are expected to launch their assault on the fighter base as we speak."

There were smiles and murmurs of appreciation around the table.

All eyes turn to Gallant as he said, "Our Hawkeye search teams have discovered sensor arrays, and our space wing has been guided around them. In addition, they identified planetary military targets for Lieutenant Ryan's strike."

Fletcher continued, "The space wing should be reaching Gliese-Beta at this very moment. It will be sometime before we will receive the code word for whether the strike achieved surprise."

"Sir are there any assessment reports?" asked Captain Ramsey.

"We can't expect that information yet, but we have not noticed any traffic pattern changes in the Titan commercial ships. And there is nothing alarming on their communication stations yet."

Gallant found it impossible to guess about the emotional state of his officers from their holographs. The ships were close enough so that there was little time-delay from the transmission, but the image quality was not the best. He assumed that they were tired and anxious, but still enthusiastic for the mission.

He had one item of news to share.

"A Hawkeye has discovered the location of the Titans' Home Fleet. And one interesting piece of information we've been able to glean is that Admiral Zzey is in command. We met him before at Ross. He's a sharp wily leader. We will have to be especially skillful to fool him. But fool him we must if we're going to carry out our part of this battle."

Heads nodded.

"We can't hope to defeat his fleet in a straight-up battle without our space wing."

With nearly all his starfighters attacking Gliese-Beta, Gallant's carriers were almost impotent.

"Our intelligence estimates he has six carriers."

He spent a moment reflecting on his battlecruisers.

"And we can't hope to defeat Zzey in a straight slugging match. A dozen capital ships are too many for the *Indefatigable* and *Indomitable,* no matter how heroic they fight. No disrespect meant to Captain Ramsey or Captain Hernandez."

Gallant gave a little wave of his hand, and the two captains returned a slight bow with a smile.

"So, what role is left for our task force?" asked Ramsey.

There was something in their eyes he wasn't comfortable with.

They expect brilliance.

"I think we should hit targets of opportunity," offered Hernandez.

"Outstanding suggestion, Captain," said Gallant. "That's exactly what we will do. We will wave a red flag in front of Admiral Zzey. We will make feints against the outer planets. Hopefully, once the enemy fleet becomes aware of our actions, they will come charging at us instead of the Marines or Lieutenant Ryan's space wing."

A silence hung in the conference room as each officer adjusted his thinking to this information.

He said, "We should use this time to discuss what targets and actions can be the most provocative with the least cost to us."

Turnbull gave Gallant a harsh look. "Look at what we're facing."

She pointed to the wall-length viewscreen, which showed the position and velocity vectors of thousands of ships.

"Unfortunately, this display is an accurate portrayal of our dilemma," she said, "How can we strike a target to effectively distract Admiral Zzey and avoid being tracked by those travelers?"

Gallant gave the group of officers a critical look. They were young, so was he, but his maturity had come from the battlefield. "Since D-Day has already started, time is not on our side. We cannot attack them directly, nor can we expect to strike and then steal away and hide."

Turnbull growled, "That's what we can't do. *Now* tell us what we *can* do."

"We *can* select a target to strike that will hurt but will suggest we are only one of several task forces in the star system—that will cause Zzey to remain on guard to protect his home world rather than chase Ryan or the Marines."

Turnbull was not placated. "What target is that?"

He turned to the theater of officers and said, "This is where you officers get to shine. Find a target that fulfills our need and send me your approach vectors as well as your assessments of the enemy's reaction. I'll reconvene this conference in six hours to compare suggestions."

There were a few startled looks and many eager faces.

"Dismissed."

Gallant waited. With nearly all the starfighters in the attack on Gliese-Beta, his carriers were virtually impotent. His battlecruisers could scarcely hope to engage the half-dozen dreadnaughts of the Titan home fleet. The best he could hope to do was lure the Titan fleet away and keep their attention on him instead of on the starfighters and Marines.

What will Admiral Zzey do?

He tapped a button and said, "Have Midshipman Logan report to my stateroom."

A few minutes later, bright eager Logan entered.

Gallant said, "Logan, I have some simulations I'd like you to run."

"Yes, sir."

"What do you think that Admiral Zzey will do?"

"Me, sir?"

"Yes, I'm asking for your opinion because you need to understand what kind of simulation assumptions to make."

"Oh. I see. Well, I guess Zzey has three problems to deal with."

"Which are?"

"First, he will want to protect Gliese-Beta from further attacks by getting between our task force and the planet."

Gallant nodded.

Logan perked up at the approval. "Then he will launch strikes against this task force, the Marines, and the withdrawing starfighters whenever he gets in range."

"And?"

"There's more, sir?"

"Yes."

Logan remained puzzled for a minute until Gallant said, "He'll want to keep his fleet together. He'll be reluctant to send large splinter forces to attack separately."

"Because he doesn't know if we have more forces hiding somewhere!" said Logan, his eyes growing wide and his mouth opening in triumph.

"Exactly. We must act aggressively to keep him guessing about our full strength. So long, as he feels threatened, the starfighters and Marines will have a chance to escape."

But deducing the enemy's intention was no guarantee they could prevail against him.

Gallant examined the star charts and contemplated his current options and their consequences. His initial plans were based on a successful surprise attack. Now he worried he was too ambitious, and things might already be unraveling. Yet, what could he do now to improve the basic plan?

It was his plan. He pushed for it. If it failed, many would die. It would be a failure he would have to live with—a wave of guilt flooded over him.

He gave several target options to Logan.

Logan said, "I can run a series of simulations testing these feints that might distract Zzey." He added, "Without giving him a hammer to stomp us."

"Yes. That will do."

Logan gathered Gallant's marked-up charts and notes in

preparation for the mockups.

"What's wrong?" asked Gallant. "You seem upset. Are you concerned about the coming battle?"

Logan's face turned into a prune as he pulled his chin and furrowed his brows. "Of course not, sir. I never worry about those kinds of things."

"Then what's troubling you?"

"I don't want to bother you with my personal problems, sir."

"It's my job to take care of my people. Is there a family problem? Are your parents ill? What's wrong?"

Logan hung his head and reluctantly said, "Her name is Katrina, but I call her Kat because she reminds me of a sleek, playful feline. She's the most wonderful girl in the world."

Gallant sighed. "I'm not the right person to discuss personal relationships. Can I set up an appointment with the XO for you?"

Logan recoiled, blanching. "Oh, no, no thank you, sir! Really. I'd rather talk to you."

"Well, go on then."

"I've had a crush on her for years. We dated for a while, but she broke up with me before we left port."

"Did she explain why?"

"There's this guy at home. She's crazy about him. Just mention his name, and she melts."

Gallant patted him on the shoulder. "You can't *make* her love you."

Logan's face fell. "Is that all, sir?"

"I know it's hard to accept, but someday you'll find someone who will love you as much as you love her. You must be patient. Sometimes it takes time."

As Gallant said the words, Alaina's image rose in his mind and he felt a surge of sorrow.

So far away.

Six hours after dismissing them, Gallant reconvened his officers around the conference table once more.

Gallant held the simulation studies that he and Logan had explored. He waited to see what his officers had uncovered.

Captain Ramsey said, "I've got the perfect target."

He inserted data into the wall video screen to illustrate his idea.

"It's a major mining colony at the edge of the asteroids. It's an important financial resource. It's poorly guarded, at least the drone reports don't show many defenses. There are few military ships nearby, but there's a load of commercial traffic moving ore. We could destroy a lot of those ships and make a real nuisance of ourselves. Zzey will become quickly aware of us, but if he comes after us, there is an easy path to the edge of the system where we can escape and warp home."

He looked proud of his plan.

Another officer said, "I have a similar idea on one of the

commercial mining stations a little deeper into the field."

Gallant heard several more proposals, but they were similar.

Turnbull said, "These are reasonable possibilities. They make a feint to attract the Titan Home Fleet and still give us an opportunity to make good our escape."

Gallant said, "Unfortunately, these plans fail to meet our most important goal."

Frowns emerged all around the table. Skepticism showed on the faces of the more senior officers.

"We must do more than a smack. We must hurt the Titans so that there is no chance they can ignore us and go after our more vulnerable starfighters and Marines."

Ramsey said, "My proposal is more than a smack."

"I don't wish to diminish any of the ideas proposed, but Admiral Zzey will recognize if we are not fully committed. He will see that our task force is making a feint. Then he will be free to crush our starfighters and Marine."

Some faces began to show understanding.

"Zzey must believe that this task force is unafraid of his fleet—that it is going to attack major facilities, at will. We have to convince him that the United Planets attacked this star system with overwhelming force and that the strike on Gliese-Beta was only the opening round—that there is more to come."

"What do you hope to accomplish by that?" asked Turnbull.

"I believe Zzey will be constrained to act defensively. He

will keep the bulk of his fleet whole and remain near Gliese-Beta. Then he will be able to launch only limited strikes at our forces."

"Captain Gallant, what target do you propose that will accomplish this?" asked Turnbull.

Gallant licked his lips. "Gliese-Alpha."

Surprise swept the table.

Turnbull looked at him askew. "You propose to attack the second most populous planet without any element of surprise? Without any starfighters?"

She threw up her hands. "Moving toward the innermost planet in this system would bring us nose to nose with the Titan Home Fleet. We would be accelerating inbound toward the sun and creating terrific momentum that we could not easily stop and reverse. It would allow the Titans an opportunity to cut off our avenue of retreat to the edge of the system and our ability to escape by warping away."

The silence persisted for another minute. Then she said, "That would be irresponsible suicide."

"That's exactly what Admiral Zzey would have to conclude as soon as he detected our task force closing in on Gliese-Alpha," said Gallant.

Turnbull opened her mouth and then snapped it shut.

Gallant said, "It's the only thing that will convince him that a much larger fleet is in the system that hasn't revealed itself yet. He will assume we are laying a trap for him, and he will freeze in place to await developments. He will be unable to leave Gliese-

Beta unprotected, and he will be unable to commit to attacking our starfighters or Marines. He will only be able to commit a small force to ward off Task Force 34 to stop our threat to Gliese-Alpha."

Many faces remained unconvinced.

He said, "His cautious approach will give the starfighters and Marines time to escape. We can keep Zzey distracted long enough for that. Then we will turn and run for our lives."

"Run for our lives is right," said Turnbull. "Zzey will be feasting on our bones before we can decelerate, turn around, and accelerate outbound from the system."

"That's where the simulation runs of our Midshipman Logan have come in handy."

Gallant pressed a button, and the door to the conference room opened. Logan walked in and immediately connected his tablet to the viewscreen.

"Proceed, Mister Logan," said Gallant.

Logan took a deep breath and said, "Commodore Gallant asked me to run some scenarios. I considered several cases where our task force made a dash toward Gliese-Alpha and then turned around to run out of the system without launching a strike against the planet."

He put the simulation results on the screen.

"I had to make some assumptions about the enemy's reaction and the speeds he needs to attain to catch us."

Turnbull asked, "And what were your final results?"

"Assuming that Admiral Zzey is reluctant to leave Gliese-

Beta undefended, I estimated that he will send a task force of roughly Task Force 34's strength after us. If that force doesn't immediately turn and chase us at greater than 0.25 C at this point here," he pointed to a location on his chart. "Then, we have a 50% chance of escaping the star system with only moderate damage to a few ships after a brief encounter with the enemy."

Turnbull said, "What?!"

Gallant said, "Acceptable risk and losses considering what we will achieve."

Ramsey said, "Sir, I should warn you that achieving warp escape velocity will be impossible with an enemy fleet hammering at our engines."

"I know it will be tight. That's why I had so many simulations run. To have the data when the circumstances arise."

Hernandez said, "But allowing the Titan fleet to get that close will mean they could launch their entire space wing at us. It would be overwhelming."

"They will never launch a full wing at us. They will always be afraid of the rest of the Third Fleet. They should be able to identify us as the same task force they faced in Ross, and they will want to search for the rest of the fleet. It will restrain them."

Wilcox, the commander of the cruiser, *Helix*, said, "There are delaying tactics that are possible such as sending a cruiser destroyer squadron to bombard local mining colonies along the way. That will cause them to wonder about other forces."

Gallant said, "That's a good idea."

"You never offered any of this analysis prior to the start of Operation Damocles," said Turnbull cutting him short.

"I always said there would be some improvisation necessary once we were in the star system and had to adjust to the situation as we found it. Assess and adapt, as the Marines like to say."

The officers murmured their satisfaction with the plan.

Satisfied that he had the officer's support, he said, "Dismissed."

After the holograms vanished, an unhappy Captain Turnbull left the conference room.

As Gallant went to the bridge and changed course toward Gliese-Alpha, he remained uncertain of Turnbull's intentions.

CHAPTER 29

Missile Lock

Ryan led a strung-out space wing away from Gliese-Beta. Of the original one hundred and sixty-two starfighters, there were only one hundred and six remaining. Forty-one fighters and fifty-four bombers were working their way forward. Another eleven damaged ships followed behind. Even with the success of Thunder and Lightning, the starfighters had already paid a high price. And they were still a long way from home.

Ryan worked with his AI feverishly trying to calculate the optimal trajectories so that his ships could reach a stable formation without losing distance to the pursuing Titans.

"It's just not possible to get the main body together without leaving the stragglers behind," he muttered to himself.

Those stragglers are going to be a problem.

He recalled Captain Gallant's words, "Getting in is going to be easier than getting out."

He was so right!

Letting his mind wander, he noticed, Ensign Joe Flannery was off course.

He said on tac1, "Bear, you're veering to port."

Ensign Samuel Rhodes was also misaligned.

"Dusty, stay tight," he admonished.

Finally, he became angry when his own wingman, Glenn Holman, was flying sloppy.

"Duck! Explain how you can be out of position when you are the leader's wingman."

"Sorry, Lucky, I got distracted."

Duck got his call sign during training when it was discovered that his antimissiles frequently missed—leaving him a sitting duck.

Ryan continued to assess the situation. He calculated that there were over four hundred fighters flushed from Gliese-Beta trailing him. They were gaining ground on the stragglers fast.

He identified another formation of over a hundred fighters coming from somewhere to his starboard, but they were still far off. He dismissed them for the time being.

Then he identified another hundred fighters on his radar coming from his port side. They would be a problem if he turned in that direction.

He adjusted the space wing's course to maneuver away

from the threats and still reach their rendezvous point with the Great Ship.

"Lucky! Sorry to be the bearer of bad news," interrupted Werewolf, "but take a look at your long-range sensors at 000 relative,"

Ryan scanned the field directly ahead of his rag-tag group. He didn't like what he saw.

Werewolf said, "The Marines let a few through."

Over fifty Phantoms were in front of the space wing. They were in a ragged dispersed order as if they had taken off at different times without controlled coordination. Still, there was a bunch of enemy fighters standing in the way, and Ryan wasn't pleased.

"How did those bastards get past the Marines?" asked Duck.

Ryan said, "I'll bet there were a lot more of them before the Marines found them."

"Well, what are we going to do now, Lucky?"

Ryan wanted to say, "Don't ask me! I haven't a clue." But, of course, he couldn't. He spent several minutes mumbling with his AI. He said, "Dusty, you take charge of the remaining fighters. Create a spearhead formation and punch a hole through the Phantoms in front of us."

"Will do, Lucky."

"Lorelei, move your bombers behind Dusty."

"Aye aye, Wing Commander."

Ryan said, "Werewolf, Duck, Bear, execute a one-eighty, and

follow me. We're going to give those stragglers some breathing room."

Ryan and his three associates formed between the stragglers and the most advanced pursuing Titans.

He was already regretting his decision when the enemy fired several long-range missiles at his little band.

They evaded the missiles, but another volley from the Titans headed toward the stragglers. Ryan was stunned when one of the stragglers took a direct hit and broke into pieces right before his eyes. He spun his small band around, bringing their full antimissile salvo to cover the stragglers.

Their crossfire decimated the Titan threat, and the stragglers kept moving.

Ryan ignored his receding space wing and concentrated his efforts on stopping the Titan lead fighters.

He weaved through the enemy leaders, striking blow after blow with his plasma and laser weapons. As more and more Phantoms closed in, he fought a desperate battle.

He ordered, "Keep tight on me."

For a moment, it looked like some Titan fighters would catch the stragglers, but then two of Ryan's band broke up the attack.

The Phantoms launched a missile barrage. For several minutes, the United Planets' ships were in turmoil, adjusting to the incoming missiles. Ryan coordinated his antimissile swarm to defend the formation. It was an effort for him to concentrate. He could only compel his mind by sheer will. He was tense, but he had bought breathing space for the stragglers. They were limping off, out of range of the Titan forces, given new life for the time being.

The battle raged around him, but Ryan caught sight of one Phantom that was wreaking havoc. It had destroyed two Vipers already and was zeroing in a bomber when Ryan alerted the pilot.

"There's a hotshot pilot on your tail."

Duck said, "I'll get that 'Red Baron.'"

Duck swooped in and made a pass at the Phantom. He fired a missile, but it missed.

A moment later, the bomber was hit and exploded.

The Red Baron turned toward Duck and sent a missile his way.

Duck launched an antimissile, but it missed. The Red Baron's missile chased Duck for less than a minute before Duck's ship was hit and damaged. He became a straggler himself.

Ryan turned to help. "Stay clear. I'll take care of this Red Baron.

Riding an adrenaline rush, he sliced through space in 'Lucky 7.' Spinning on his gyro, he ignited an extra thruster to drive the engine hotter. He came around to get a bead on the Red Baron, but the Phantom slipped away.

Damn. He's good.

Several iridescent obscenities escaped his mouth in rapid succession as his pulse raced.

He moved his ship to get a better attack angle, but in the high-G turn, he felt the crush of g's press against his chest.

Once more, the Red Baron blew by him. He watched the ship roar away as if Lucky 7 was in slow motion. He curved back toward him for another pass. With thrusters already at max burn, he punched the afterburner.

He lost track of the Red Baron, and in mere seconds the Titan maneuvered behind him.

He tried to shake him but couldn't.

He blanched, but his brain was already calculating the pros and cons. He knew a good thing when he saw it and a bad one when he heard it. And his ideas in the middle of a battle were mostly bad.

"Damn!" he screamed as the other ship twisted with him turn for turn.

Despite his frustration, he allowed himself a faint smile at the Red Baron's expertise.

Ryan pressed back into his seat, turning just in time to avoid a missile. He flinched, then gritted his teeth. The battle began to slip away from his grasp when a near-miss explosion jarred his Viper. Ryan shook his head.

He closed his eyes again, willing the dizziness to leave while he pulled his neural interface back into position.

"Lucky! Lucky! What happened?" asked Duck.

"I'm . . . Okay. I'm Okay," Ryan stammered somewhat disoriented. Restoring his mental picture through the neural interface, he recognized ships and their trajectories.

The Red Baron stuck with him, move for move. He chased him and kept close on Ryan's six.

The cockpit warning lights lit up the cabin as Ryan dodged.

RADAR SCAN!

RADAR SCAN!

His radar warning alerted.

MANEUVER TO AVOID LOCK-ON!

MANEUVER TO AVOID LOCK-ON!

He used every bit of expertise he could muster to twist, turn, and wrestle his jet into an escape angle from the trailing Phantom.

Ryan flew like a maniac. He wondered if Lucky 7 would hold together. The engine sputtered, complaining of the abusive application of power and radical course change. When he heard warning messages from the AI, he was forced to ease up on the relentless thrust he applied.

Panic tugged at his awareness. He couldn't sense anything over the confusion that churned in his head. He had missed the Red Baron.

Where is he?

Ryan queried his AI.

"Target is on the starboard quarter."

"Oh no, you don't!" exclaimed Ryan, "You're not getting behind me again."

He pulled back on the stick. He spun his gyros and reversed

course one hundred and eighty degrees before lighting his engines off again at maximum. A trick he had learned from his mentor, Henry Gallant.

His ship pivoted and swung around so violently that his vision narrowed into a tunnel, and he had a grey-out. He finally had target acquisition, and a moment later, he was tracking.

With semi-awareness, he heard the AI report, "Missile lock-on target."

Ryan pressed the trigger. Then he pressed it again.

"Missiles away," reported the AI.

Ryan weaved in and out of mental focus as his ship steadied on course, and the g-forces on his chest lessened.

A blinding flash covered his viewport for several seconds, and the AI reported, "Target destroyed."

Ryan's head bobbled back and forth. He tried to grasp what had happened.

"Did I hit the Red Baron?"

"Target destroyed," repeated the AI.

"Damn straight!"

The Lucky 7 flew level for another few minutes without incident while Ryan collected his wits.

The Titan pursuit was now far behind.

Ryan went over tac 1 and asked, "Dusty, how are you doing?"

Dusty replied, "I'm kind of busy right now, but I wouldn't complain if you sprinted up to the front of the formation and helped out."

CHAPTER 30

Raining Fire

Steward was six days shy of his twenty-sixth birthday, and he lay filthy and exhausted in a bombed-out trench filled with equally grimy Marines. Bullets buzzed passed like mosquitoes, and his rapid breathing fogged up his facemask.

He recognized that at this point, he didn't have any good options. Able and Charlie company were nearly surrounded and grossly outnumbered. His remaining companies were pinned down by artillery fire, and he had no idea where his rescue ship, the *Warrior*, was.

Sonny burst into the ditch and nearly fell on top of him. Sonny was bleeding from a laser blast that seared his shoulder, but he was still yelling at the top of his lungs, "Is that all you got! Is that all you got! Come on. I'm waiting for ya'."

He slammed his rifle into the ground. He had an abusive relationship with the weapon ever since it jammed during the last scuffle—forcing him to fight hand-to-hand with a beefy Titan. He ended up with plenty of bruises and a few laser burns.

He slammed the gun down again. He wasn't the forgiving type.

McCauley grabbed hold of him and sat him down. He applied a patch over his bloody shoulder.

"Easy, Sonny. You've got plenty of time. We'll save a few for you."

"Damn! I wish Pappy were here," said Sonny, with a rasp in his throat.

Sergeant Ernest 'Pappy' Papias had become a legend since his heroic action a year earlier, and for a moment, Steward wondered what 'Pappy' *would do* if he were there.

He said, "I miss him too, Sonny."

"I meant no disrespect, sir. I'm sure you know what to do. It was just that Pappy always knew what to say to make me believe everything was going to be alright."

"If he were here now, he would say, 'Just keep shooting!'"

Sonny nodded. "Yeah. He would."

WEEEEEEE!!!

Steward cursed at the unnerving screech of an enemy rocket launcher. He wanted to reassess the defensive perimeter, but he was unable to connect to Charlie company's AR network.

"Come with me. I've got to get to the Charlie company commander."

The Marines left the ditch and lurched forward. An augmented reality image showed above his right eye, giving him the terrain and location data for Able company personnel. As he moved, he sought cover in boulders and crevasses within the topsy-turvy combat environment. Throwing a grenade, he crept forward, looking for cover behind a mound of volcanic rocks.

Brilliant flashes of plasma weapons shrieked past him and struck a nearby boulder.

He came to an outcropped ledge, and he fired. As he leveled his weapon again, he spotted several aliens coming his way.

Thpff! Thpff! Thpff!

He ducked low to avoid the heavy weapon fire.

A moment later, he fired back.

Pfft! Pfft! Pfft!

With all the bravado he could muster, he thrust himself forward and fired. He killed two. Firing at more vague figures, he moved and fired again.

Pfft! Pfft! Pfft!

He tossed a grenade but lost his footing and fell.

Sonny and McCauley leaped from boulder to boulder keeping close behind him.

Nearby blinding flashes of plasma weapons streaked past him

WEEEEEEE!!!

Steward thought, *for sheer irritation, that sound can't be beat.*

Finally, he found the Charlie company commander and asked, "Where's the rest of your company?"

"You're looking at it," he said, pointing to three dozen men lying on their bellies around him.

Pling! Pling! Pling!

Bullets ricocheted nearby.

Steward reorganized the Charlie company men into a stronger defensive position.

"McCauley! Get a machine gun set on that outcropping," said Steward pointing to a dominating position.

A few minutes later, a welcomed sound arrived.

Dat-dat-dat-dat-dat-dat-dat-dat-dat-dat!

A nearby explosion sent shrapnel hurtling toward Steward. Through the debris, he saw flashes and explosions. He fell hard to the ground. He felt his body to find the injuries. His hands were the worst.

"Are you alright?" asked McCauley crawling next to him.

What he wanted to say was, "How can I be alright when everything around me is trying to kill me?" but despite his burns and injuries, he lied, "I'm fine. Fine."

Steward vomited blood into his mask.

McCauley shook his head and called on tac1, "Medic? I need a medic."

It took several minutes before a medic could work his way to Steward.

"He has several bad injuries," said the medic.

McCauley said, "Better give him a strong painkiller."

Steward protested, "No. I need to keep a clear head."

A faint thought formed in his mind. Something about his position locator and communication device.

What was it?

His brain screamed. He needed to contact the *Warrior*.

Where are they?

Steward said, "Sergeant, send a distress signal to the *Warrior*."

CHAPTER 31

Engage

The Constellation surged through the asteroid field, every second getting closer to Gliese-Alpha, the second most populous planet in the system.

She was a wolf amongst the flock. Ship after ship was overhauled, and a shot, or two, from a laser, or a railgun, was adequate to convince the crew to abandon ship. Then a single missile was enough to destroy the freighter.

The Titan communication networks were alive with alarm as the shocked merchants sought to escape—few did. The task force's presence in the area was now known. Its light reached many ships and sensor arrays. Hundreds of commercial ships were fleeing before them.

Gallant wanted to inflict the greatest damage possible, and he fumed with every delay.

Six light-hours away from the planet, he was standing on the bridge when he received, "Thunder! Thunder! Thunder!"

Cheers broke out on the bridge.

Fletcher said, "The first broadcasts coming from the Gliese-Beta news media claim that the attacks were massive. After that, I'm sure the government censors took over. The attack was then characterized as mild with minimal damage, obviously looking to reassure the public."

Turnbull said, "But their military got the actual reports. That news, along with these raids on the asteroid shipping lanes, should give the Titans a lot to think about."

"Sir, we're being identified by a sensor array. Request permission to destroy it," asked the OOD.

"Negative. We want Zzey to know who and where we are. Let him stew with that information."

CIC reported, "We are picking up communications between the Titan high command and their fleet, but it's encoded, and we can't translate."

Fletcher said, "I'll bet the government is getting on Zzey's case about preventing us from reaching another planet."

"If it were our government, they would."

Gallant ordered, "OOD arrange a task force video conference. I want every senior commanding officer to attend."

"Aye aye, sir."

Gallant went to the video conference room and took his place at the podium along with Fletcher and Turnbull.

The OOD opened a channel and said, "Commodore, all commanding officers are present on-line."

Gallant looked around the table at the three-dimensional hologram.

"Officers, we have received the messages, 'Thunder' and 'Lightning.'"

The officers applauded and cheered.

"Our disruption of the Titan commerce has also not gone unnoticed. Every communication network inside the star system is alive with the news."

Once more, the officers exchanged joyful congratulations.

"We have one drone near Gliese-Alpha that reports their battle stations and fighter CSP are on full alert awaiting our arrival."

He paused. "They will be disappointed we will not come knocking."

The faces looked at him, expectant of more urgent news.

"Admiral Zzey . . .," he began. Taking his time, he licked his lips and said, "has reacted in line with one of our scenarios."

"He has moved his fleet close to Gliese-Beta to forestall a second attack. He is still within striking range of our Marines in the asteroids, and our retreating starfighters heading toward point ZED."

Looking around the table, he saw many troubled faces.

"Then he hasn't taken our bait to come after us?"

"I didn't say that. He has split a task force off from his Home

Fleet and sent it this way."

"Then, we failed."

"No, we haven't. We accomplished our main goal. He has kept most of his forces intact and close to Gliese-Beta. He's still hesitating while he conducts long-range searches. I think our starfighters and Marines will escape a direct assault from his fleet."

"What about this task force he's sending toward us?"

"We managed to get a drone near it. Before it was destroyed, it identified the task force of one carrier and four dreadnaughts sent to intercept us before we reach Gliese-Alpha."

"Then we should turn around immediately and head out of the system. We've accomplished what we could. Now it's time to leave," said Turnbull.

"Not quite. I said Zzey was hesitating to go after the Marines. It's still possible he could get them before the Warrior retrieves them. We have to maintain our ruse a little while longer."

Turnbull shook her head. "No. Look at the trajectories on the video screen. The Titan task force is accelerating away from the sun while we are accelerating toward it. Their velocity will give them the ability to catch us if we don't turn immediately."

"Not yet."

The Titan admiral knew his business. Zzey sacrificed distance to gain on the angle of approach toward the task force. Mathematically, he was in the perfect position to protect Gliese-Beta and threaten them.

Gallant said, "Almost certainly, he will assume that we would only attack these planets with a fleet as large as his own. But so far, he's only got a whiff of our two carriers. I suspect that Admiral Zzey is making a tough decision right about now. In the end, he will strike with a bombing run from his one carrier."

Turnbull said, "So, you figure he'll send forty or fifty bombers at us."

"More likely, thirty," he said.

"We only have six fighters remaining for CSP."

"Our combat patrol will be enough to keep them guessing and off-balance. We should be able to weather that storm. We'll keep our fingers crossed that our point defense will save us from major damage."

Gallant had placed the task force in a precarious position. They were close enough to threaten Gliese-Alpha, but their momentum was sunward. Zzey's task force was accelerating toward the task force away from the sun. For the task force to turn around and run from the sun, they would have to brake and reaccelerate. Zzey might catch them before they could escape.

The *Constellation's* long-range sensors and the input from several drones showed that the Titans were closing.

An operator reported, "Sir, long-range sensors are picking up velocity vectors from the enemy. They are altering course to intercept us."

The task forces were ten light-minutes apart.

As the ships closed, something felt wrong.

A minute later, Gallant ordered, "All ships, execute formation Alpha Seven. I repeat, execute Alpha Seven."

A few minutes later, the OOD reported, "We are picking up a large flight of Titan bombers."

Captain Turnbull said, "I advise you to turn around and run from this star system now while we can."

Gallant said, "No. Accepting battle at the time and place of our choosing is our best option. It all comes down to timing. Given the relativistic effects, making changes too early will give the enemy time to react. On the other hand, if we're too late, the ships will never reach the proper position."

He was setting out on the most reckless gamble of his life, and danger be damned, he was in command. So, he was startled when Turnbull said, "Captain Gallant, I remind you that I am senior."

It was a devastating point. One that he had not considered seriously until this moment. If she chose, Turnbull could relieve him and take command herself, despite his pro temp appointment as Commodore. No doubt, there would be a great deal of gnashing of teeth when they returned to Melbourne. She would be hard-pressed to justify his removal without showing a clear violation of his duty. Yet, the word 'senior' seemed to linger in the air.

Later in life, Gallant might look upon this moment with some perspective. He could come to realize that this moment might divert his destiny in one or another direction. He might recall all the near-death experiences he escaped, circumstances where 'all seemed to be lost,' and then fate took a hand and saved him. Perhaps, saved him for this very instant.

Gallant turned his head to one side. He looked at Turnbull as if trying to see her from a different perspective.

"It was thoughtless of me not to give your suggestion the complete consideration it deserved. I beg your pardon."

She didn't respond.

He said, "Officers, dismissed."

The holograms of the ship's officers vanished, and Fletcher left. But Turnbull remained.

He said, "Captain, you're in the most awkward position. You're sitting in the back seat, wishing you could get your hands on the steering wheel. You think you could make each turn sharper and closer to the wall. You feel that everything would be better served under your direction."

He paused and leaned closer to her, nose to nose.

"You doubt me. It's only normal that you should want control. But we couldn't be in a worse predicament, and I am the source of that. What's your solution? Do you want the burden of fighting this battle and explaining the results, assuming we live to face Admiral Graves afterward?"

She almost nodded but caught herself.

"Agatha, I ask you to put aside your desire for command. I ask you to forget about pleasing Admiral Graves, to forget that I am not genetically engineered and that you dislike me personally."

He took hold of her arm and said, "I want you to believe that you can trust me to make the best decisions under these circumstances."

He squeezed her arm. He whispered, "Trust me."

She stood there, not moving for what seemed a long time. She blinked, but she did not attempt to pull away from his grip.

In the end, he couldn't be sure if she had relented because she was convinced that he would be the one to succeed, or because she feared to accept the responsibility for herself.

But finally, she said, "I never said that I disliked you, Henry."

He smiled.

She asked, "Is there anything I can do to help?"

"Of course. You could go to CIC and evaluate the fighting weaknesses of the enemy fleet."

"Yes, Commodore."

She marched to CIC while Gallant went to the bridge.

"The enemy formation consists of thirty-six bombers and twelve fighters," said the sensor operator.

Gallant said, "Launch all fighters."

There were only six fighters left to protect the *Constellation*, but they would have to do.

Minutes later, the report came, "They're closing to weapons range."

As the bombers began their missile runs, Gallant unleashed a barrage of antimissiles.

"Will the antimissiles stop them?" asked Turnbull.

"Not all of them."

Gallant ordered the task force into a tight formation with overlapping point defenses to repel bombers. He ordered the six fighters to ignore their counterparts and drive at the bombers.

It's time, he thought and turned the task force around. They were now accelerating away from the sun.

Even before the enemy released their first missile, Gallant released countermeasures.

The support ships moved to station themselves between the enemy and the carriers for the greatest protection. He watched the ships move into position. The bombers damaged several ships, but the task force emerged intact.

"The enemy is adjusting its task force formation. The carrier has been identified as the *Vampiri*," said the OOD.

Feeling a tightness in his gut, Gallant watched the enemy's threat become real. "That's the flagship. Zzey has left the bulk of his fleet to guard Gliese-Beta while he is leading this task force against us."

He gritted his teeth, surprised at this development. He was unsure about what to do next as the enemy began reacting to his formation.

"They're still closing fast. It takes ten minutes for them to see what we've done."

Gallant found himself wishing that the Third Fleet was really in the star system.

Three-dimensional warfare in space is geometrically constrained by the gravity field. He kept a close watch on the position and momentum vectors.

He used the time to fight off the bombers and turn the task force away and headed toward the system edge. Finally, Task Force 34 was running away from the Titan force, but the maneuver slowed them down and gave the enemy a chance to close the distance.

Their mission completed the Titan bombers left. But now the enemy dreadnaughts were closing in. The capital ships made an initial charge without fancy maneuvers.

Their first missile barrage was not very effective due to United Planets' decoys and massive point defenses. But the second barrage was more effective facing fewer defenses.

One destroyer's shield collapsed, and it exploded.

The next pass was a brutal exchange of fire. The grapeshot and lasers slapped and rocked the ships. Some shields buckled and then collapsed.

The dreadnaughts were moving much faster than Task Force 34. Gallant feared that he had cut his escape too fine—that Zzey had reacted quicker than he anticipated.

Each minute showed the multicolored velocity vectors flickering as Task Force 34 fled. The dreadnaughts were already at high velocity.

Gallant sat grim-faced as the distance narrowed with each second. The dreadnaughts were winning. They would reach the engagement range in minutes.

The OOD of the *Constellation* said, "I'm receiving a message from the Indomitable, sir. She said she is going to operate independently."

"What?" Gallant looked at the ship's trajectory as she turned toward the Titan formation at 0.3 C.

"*Indomitable,* this is Commodore Gallant. Return to the formation. That is an order."

"Sorry, sir. Ramsey out."

"Captain Ramsey don't do this," said Gallant, but he knew Ramsey was right. Task Force 34 was about to be cut off from escape, and only a 'Hail Mary' sacrifice could save it.

Ramsey said, "Some of us are going to die, but this ship can make a difference. I am confident my crew shares my commitment."

The OOD said, "Commodore, the *Indomitable* is heading into the enemy's line of advance."

The *Indomitable* did the impossible. She disrupted the enemy formation, which deteriorated into chaos as she plunged through it.

Gallant received reports of the blow by blow destruction of the battle cruiser. She took hits from missiles, plasma cannons, and lasers. The engines held on until she was inside the Titan formation. Then the kinetic rounds started to penetrate her hull.

Her shield buckled, and her hull lit up bright red from the plasma and laser weapons bouncing off the titanium hull.

But she wasn't helpless. She fired every weapon she had and sent missile after missile at the enemy ships. One cruiser exploded in her path, and a dreadnaught took direct hits in its engine room, forcing it to pull out of formation.

The *Indomitable* became silent.

Gallant fought a rising sense of fear, wondering how badly the *Indomitable* was hurt.

Where is Ramsey?

The *Indomitable* spasmed as air streamed out.

"Maybe she'll survive," said the helmsman.

The enemy ships tangled with her passing a few light-seconds away.

The ship was not dead yet. But she was dying.

Gallant put his hand over his eyes. He wasn't the only one.

He was guilty of bringing all these sailors to this fate. He wouldn't let that sacrifice go to waste.

Gallant knew exactly what it was like aboard the Indomitable—the collapsed shields, the ruptured hull, the broken bulkheads, the leaking air, the last gasps of the crew. He knew the impact of weapons striking without mercy or end. He had experienced all that when the *Intrepid* was attacked at Tau Ceti.

"The *Indomitable* is launching escape pods," reported the OOD.

The battle was now sixty light-seconds away from the *Constellation*. The displays showed images a minute old.

The enemy ships swamped around the *Indomitable*.

Soon, the inevitable happened. The *Indomitable* began to break into pieces, and then containment failure led to a catastrophic explosion.

The bridge console beeped with signals coming from escape pods. He gazed at the wreckage strewn in space.

There was nothing he could do to help them now. Those survivors would soon be at the mercy of the Titans.

The Titan fleet passed the broken hull of the *Indomitable* and collected itself, trying to restore order to their formation.

Gallant was busy leading his remaining ships toward escape by accelerating out of the star's gravity well. Every second he gained was a chance for the task force to survive. He wanted to make the heroic sacrifice of those aboard the Indomitable pay off for the rest of the task force.

As they gathered velocity, driving away from the star, Gallant said, "I don't think there was any other way for us to escape. I commend Captain Ramsey and his crew."

The Titan fleet was now behind falling behind the task force. It was organizing itself for pursuit, but with each passing second, Task Force 34 was opening the distance. It would stay ahead of Zzey until it reached the star system edge.

They prepared to warp out of the star system.

CHAPTER 32

Tethered

Steward watched as the last of the Phantoms flew off the asteroid. He wondered what he could do to stop them.

It was too late.

The space wing will have to fend for itself.

He felt a twinge of pain from his wound and pressed his hand to his side. The medic told him to rest, but that was impossible. He had to get his Marines off this godforsaken asteroid.

First things, first.

He had to clear a landing zone, but his depleted Marines needed help.

He signaled the *Warrior* to send Cobras to his coordinates. The Cobras flew to the battlefront with their high caliber Gatling guns blazing. They churned up the soil and killed a lot of Titans.

"McCauley take a squad and outflank them. You others

come with me."

McCauley formed a dozen Marines into a line a hundred meters to the west. They knelt and aimed at the approaching Titans coming over the ridgeline. At the sight of the row of soldiers, the Titans hesitated.

"Aim," shouted McCauley, his hoarse voice cracked.

"Grab the tethers and attached the wounded," shouted Steward as he tried to carry out the evacuation amid a hail of Titan gunfire.

"Now, Sergeant! Give it to them."

"Fire!" said the sergeant.

It was an effective volley and it made the Titans pull back to the other side of the ridge.

"Come on!" yelled Steward. "Get the wounded out of here."

The Cobras lifted off, pulling tethers with wounded bound up in secure sacks.

The weight of the sacks caused the machines to weave as they headed up to the *Warrior*.

By the time they returned, the Titans had regained their courage, and once more were over the ridge.

One Cobra swooped down on the enemy and let its Gatling guns spew bullets into the oncoming group. It was enough to cause them to turn back yet again.

For a second, the huddled men raised their voices in derision at the scurrying Titans.

"Silence! Silence!" screamed Steward. "Pay attention to

what you're doing."

The other Cobras spread their tethers and collected a necklace of Marines.

Most of the Marines were evacuated at this point, and Steward concentrated on getting his rearguard out.

"Sonny, secure the east end of the landing zone perimeter."

Sonny manned a machine gun to cover the ravine approaches. It was the first time, he had significant responsibility. He was touchy about doing everything right.

As the last Marines were hooking up to the Cobra, he asked the pilot to direct the Gatling guns toward the hillside.

The Cobra guns tore up the landscape.

A Titan RPG fired and hit a Cobra. Its armor kept the spacejet from plummeting, but smoke billowed out of the engine, and the pilot had to make a forced landing.

The action continued for several more minutes until the Gatling guns proved their worth and drove the Titans back.

When the Titan soldiers were on the run, the Cobras dropped their tethers to gather up the remaining exhausted Marines. Flight after flight shuttled back and forth between the ships and the asteroid desperate to get all the Marines aboard before the enemy could rally and attack again.

Finally, Steward attached his own tether. He was the last to leave the asteroid.

A sudden thought struck Steward, causing him to turn and look back over his shoulder. He did a double take to see the silhouette of the hillside of the landing zone. There was movement. He could just make out Titan vehicles and soldiers swarming into the area the Marines had vacated. They were firing at the last escaping Cobras and the Marines hanging on the thin tethers. As the Cobra flew over the asteroid, another incongruous sight greeted him. He saw the remains of the fighter command center. It was smoldering. Trained construction teams would take months to rebuild that facility.

The *Warrior* was waiting for him. The last segment of the journey seemed longer than everything else. Captain Roberts welcomed him as he stepped aboard.

"Major, I'm glad to see you," said Roberts grabbing Steward's arm and helping him stand easy. "Chief get the wounded to sickbay as quickly as possible."

Steward took a few halting steps. Roberts asked, "Do you need help?"

"Actually, your arm would be welcomed."

CHAPTER 33

Better Late

Lorelei leaned forward. She put her arms on the computer console and rested her head on her arms, like a child resting her head on her school desk.

Exhausted, covered in sweat and filth, she had, for two days, kludged and coaxed her crippled Viper to trail after the fleeing starfighters just one step ahead of a thousand angry Phantoms.

She had made it to point ZED only to find ... empty space.

No Great Ship awaited her.

Hour, after hour, she waited, spiraling around a now meaningless location as the enemy came ever closer.

"Damn!" she shouted when the ship's backup power sputtered its last spark, and the tangle of makeshift wires, she had rigged, burst into flames. She dowsed the mess with a fire retardant and threw up her hands.

It was the end.

"Where the hell is that ship?" she screamed, a tear of exasperation sliding down her cheek.

And then it happened.

The space in front of her wiggled, and all the stars disappeared. It was as if a vast black hole opened and swallowed her. There was nothingness in front of her, no stars, no asteroids, no nothing.

She heard Ryan yell over tac1, "Hard to port! Max thrust! Flip gyros!"

As the remaining seventy-seven starfighters of Task Force 34's space wing attempted to execute Ryan's order—she didn't even try.

"I love you, Rob. Goodbye," were her last words as she flipped off the safety cover and pulled the emergency escape pod lever.

The pod ejected and shot to port.

Ryan looked at the wiggling black nothingness in space before him and knew exactly what it was. It was the business end of a gigantic super-laser tube.

He repeated, "Hard to port! Max thrust! Flip gyros!" and hoped the space wing would get clear in time.

How much time?

He didn't know.

Seconds passed as they changed direction to become perpendicular to the line of fire of the great weapon.

Minutes passed as they moved away from the barrel of the huge cannon.

Ryan was only slightly relieved the Great Ship had materialized at point ZED.

Better late than never.

He heard the Great Ship order, "United Planets' fighters move out of the way. Take precautions against radiation exposure."

Ryan went on tac1 and said, "All starfighters steady on course 270. Shut down all sensors and strengthen shields.

Several starfighters were trailing off in the distance followed by over a thousand Phantoms, hellbent on exacting revenge on everything before them.

Ryan waited.

Then the flash came, one tremendous burst of hellish-white energy flowed out of the super-laser.

In the blink of an eye, the laser beam was gone, but the intensity of the pulse left a red-yellow glow tapering from the tube into the space around it.

His nervous system tingled as he felt the humming lightning bolt of laser pulses coming from the Great Ship. Lucky 7 shot sparks and produced whines and grinds unlike anything ever before. Ryan shook from the vibrations around him. It was as if hell had unleashed every demon it had ever devoured. The temperature in his fighter grew so hot that his A/C unit failed, and he began sucking on a straw to his water reserves. System failures were occurring from every device in the craft. A radiation shock wave hit his ship, traveling so fast that there was no warning, and he was knocked about.

"Reinforce rear-shields," he shouted, hoping the AI would still function. "Stop all nonessential power usage."

Ryan collapsed in his seat, weak from reaction.

The energy discharge had changed the super-laser spikes extending from the Great Ship. They glowed red hot. So much heat was still radiating from them that Ryan thought the spikes squirmed against the star background.

He felt an unreality come over him. It was like being drunk.

For a long while, he sat motionless in his cockpit, his eyes burning, his ears listening to strange static sounds, his instrument panel flashing all different colors, and his AI mumbling nonsense. Pilot's reports intruded into his consciousness as they told of system failures and emergencies.

"I'm still alive," he muttered.

"Answer rollcall," he ordered.

Along with over a thousand Titan fighters, the Great Ship had managed to kill three of his pilots as well.

Secondary radiation shock waves followed, but soon normal space returned.

"That energy wave fried everything," said Dusty.

One thousand Titan fighters had vanished without a trace. The space they had occupied was void. Not even a tiny metal fragment was left to search for its own orbit around the sun.

The few remaining Phantoms, a long way off, turned away to escape.

The Great Ship opened its hangar doors, and the United Planets' starfighters began landing aboard her.

As Ryan's turn to land came, he heard the plaintiff bleeping signal of a lone escape pod's distress call.

He turned and used his tractor beam to catch the escape pod and bring Lorelei home.

Task Force 34 and the Great Ship got the hell out of the Gliese star system.

CHAPTER 34

Homeport

The Constellation 'tied up' to her moorings at the Melbourne space station. Gallant had no sooner opened the main portal for his crew to go on liberty, then Captain McCall came aboard and asked to see him in his stateroom.

She gave him a mischievous grin. "I've read your action report and seen your ship's log, but I need to get a firsthand debriefing from you for Admiral Graves. He had the kindness do it this way instead of having you report to him officially. You'll get on liberty sooner this way. I'm sure you appreciate that."

Gallant frowned as he sat down on a plush chair in his large stateroom.

McCall plopped into a stuffed chair beside him. She pulled out her tablet and tapped until she had opened to his battle report. It had multicolor notations throughout.

She nodded to Gallant.

"The operation was a success," he said. "We hit the Titans hard on Gliese-Beta, and we did severe damage to their fighter force thanks to the Great Ship. I imagine their leadership is in complete disarray, trying to put together how we accomplished the attack. I've listed special commendations for Captain Roberts, Major James Steward, and Lieutenants Lorelei Steward and Rob Ryan."

She said, "President Neumann will address the nation in a few hours to laud our great success in striking at the home world of our enemy. Admiral Graves will take a bow for the success of the Third Fleet's operation. And Captain Turnbull will be at his side to give a detailed account of the battle action."

He frowned but remained silent.

"If you could be patient just a little longer, I would like you to address a few points of contention?"

"Points of contention?"

"Several anomalies that occurred during the process of the mission that have troubled Admiral Graves. Please begin with your arrival at Gliese."

"In my report, I delineated the time evolution of the operation. The insertion of my task force began with the commitment of two stealth ships carrying a Marine battalion to a key Titan fighter base. Then Task Force 34 dispersed search drones and Hawkeyes to find sensor arrays and the Titan home fleet."

His brain began pouring information out in an organized,

logical progression of facts, issues, and data. He recognized patterns that formed solutions, and he offered his opinions.

She locked eyes with him.

"You found nothing abnormal as you proceeded with your plan?"

"We stumbled across a derelict ship, but that proved to be of no consequences."

"Admiral Graves noted that as a concern."

"In what way?"

"He suggests that it shows a lack of prudence that a genetically enhanced officer wouldn't have made."

Gallant's face contoured into complete bewilderment.

"We'll come back to this point later. For now, please proceed with your account."

"The space wing was launched according to plan, and the Marines reached their target. This is all in my report. Why must I retell it again?"

"Was it at this point that the Great Ship first appeared?"

"Oh?" he said, realizing the significance of the question. He pictured Aurora as she had stood in his stateroom—tall, majestic, dignified—her complexion changing with her mood. It pulled him back into that moment. Her mesmerizing words were as real to him now as when he first heard them. He wondered what she was doing at this moment, what setting she was in, what people she might be talking to, what plans she might be hatching. She could be in some quiet, splendid, obscure location, or flying to another star. There was no way of knowing. He sat for several minutes, enthralled in the sensation.

At length, he blinked and returned to the present

McCall remained sitting, watching him. Waiting.

"Yes. Aurora confronted me with her demands before she would carry out her part of the bargain to support the operation."

"You agreed to her terms to allow them access to the Ross system?"

"What choice did I have? She was crafty enough to make her demands at precisely the most delicate point in the operation. I had to acquiesce or face ruination."

"I understand, but Admiral Graves has identified this as another error in judgment made by a Natural."

Gallant bristled at the word Natural.

"I need to get your assessment of the Chameleon."

"Oh? Do you think that the President is interested in the opinion of a Natural?"

"Actually, this is for my personal use in compiling my SIA evaluation."

He smirked.

"What do you make of our new ally?" she asked.

Gallant had been an officer long enough and had traveled extensively enough to gauge the honor and integrity of those he had dealings with. He knew when promises were made half-heartedly—when procrastination and double-dealing played a role in an agreement.

He said, "There was a moment during the battle when I knew we had 'crossed a bridge' when the universe was altered, and I could see the future clearly. And it will not be good for humanity. I can shed light on what we must face."

"The Chameleon are not our friends," he said.

McCall did not seem surprised by this revelation.

He added, "They have not played fair with us, and they will continue to seek every advantage they can."

"I've already seen evidence of their *Ruse de guerre*," she said.

He nodded. "They are going to try to infiltrate our networks and undermine our government. They see us as a greater long-term threat than the Titans because they see us as direct competitors of oxygen planets. They might stick with us for a while to get our minerals and use our manpower, but ultimately they will betray us."

McCall made notes in her tablet. "Thank you for that frank assessment. It fits in with my own analysis."

"Are we done now? Can I go home?"

"I'm sorry, but a new law has been enacted since you were away."

"Law?"

"The Law for Human Attainment."

"That law for genetic profiling passed?"

"Yes, unfortunately. I have to ask you some questions under this law to determine your qualifications to serve in the armed forces."

She pushed a long paper form in front of him, filled with detailed personal questions about his birth and the birth of his parents. The questionnaire required a detailed listing of his DNA profile and biological imperfections.

"You must turn in the form within the next two days."

"What?"

"This is not my doing. I am only carrying out the orders I received from my superiors. This evaluation will have a bearing on the admiralties' assessment of decisions you made during the action in the Gliese star system."

"Admiral Collingsworth authorized this?" asked Gallant astonished.

"Actually, no."

She looked down and struggled to find the words to go on.

"Admiral Collingsworth is no longer Commander-in-Chief. He was removed from his post when he protested against this legislation."

Gallant sat frozen. He couldn't believe that even Neumann would be so foolhardy as to dismiss his finest military leader in order to forward a deeply misguided idea of cultural separation.

"Admiral Graves has been nominated by President Neumann to be the new Commander-in-Chief of the armed forces. Senate approval is expected to be unopposed given his victory in attacking the Titans' home planet."

"Damn them!" exclaimed Gallant, putting his hands over his ears.

Having always done his duty, he was unfit for understanding anything else. He couldn't fathom the duplicity of others. The trenchant division between right and wrong, integrity and narcissism, self-sacrifice and selfishness, had left little venue for reconciliation in his mind. He wondered what was left of the values he grew up believing.

McCall grimaced. "Don't be disheartened. George Collingsworth has joined Richard Kent's political party and announced his opposition to this administration."

She moved closer. "Things may seem terrible, but you're the kind who runs into a blazing building for the sake of others. You're the kind of man this nation needs ... and *wants*."

He pulled his hands down.

She reached out and folded his hands into hers. "Men like you are rare, but our people won't survive without them. I want you to understand that there are those like Collingsworth and Kent and me who realize that. When the chips are down, we will always rise to support you to fight for what is right. Don't count us out. We are with you. *I promise*."

They sat staring at one another for several minutes as locked in a moment of mutual understanding and commitment.

Gallant wondered what he had done to deserve such a harvest friendship and comradeship.

"Are we done now?" he asked. "If there's nothing further, I'm anxious to get home."

He started to rise.

"We're done. But you needn't worry. I spoke to Alaina only two days ago, and she was fine. Just fine," said McCall. "By the way, how is Kelsey Mitchell fitting in on the *Constellation*?"

Gallant froze. His face grew rosy.

"I only ask because her father-in-law was interested."

"She's fine," he said. "Just fine."

CHAPTER 35

Home

The moment Henry Gallant opened the door to his apartment, Alaina rushed into his arms.

"I'm so happy you're back," she said, smothering him with kisses. "I love you so much."

"I love you too," he said, overcome by a deluge of conflicting emotions. They hit him hard as she pressed against him.

For so long, he had felt lost. And now, despite her words, he sensed a reluctance . . . a hesitation from her. He wanted to believe that his capacity for self-sabotage wasn't boundless. That he still stood a chance to make things right and keep her.

He took a step back.

"What's wrong?" she asked, her face troubled.

He knew what was wrong. All of her insecurity and frustrations were clear to him now.

"You're happy to see me," he said, "but you're harboring some ill will."

She looked frightened.

He continued, "I don't blame you. You feel that my loyalty is divided, that I'm emotionally selfish and unwilling to let go of a past relationship."

Tears welled up in her eyes. "Even though all that's true, I still love you."

"You shouldn't have to keep all that bottled up inside. It will eat away at your self-esteem and foster resentment. It may have already irreparably damaged the bond between us." His voice dropped. "You may have even wished I wouldn't come back."

"Don't say that! That's not true."

But a tear slid down her cheek.

"Isn't it?"

"No. I was worried that I would lose you. More than ever before."

"Why?" Even though her pain was real, he needed to hear her reassurance.

"Well ... Kelsey was there on the ship with you. I kept asking 'what if'—if something happened to you, or if she and you ... and all the answers terrified me, and I couldn't stop crying," she said. "I do love you, more than ever. I'm hopelessly in love with you. You're a fool to think otherwise."

Gallant could see the love in her eyes. He put his fingers on her lips.

"Shhh," he said. "I love you too. You're in my arms now, and that's all that matters. Let's leave all the what ifs in the past—where they belong.

    THE END

FROM THE AUTHOR

I hope you enjoyed this book. I must confess, I'm proud of my characters and the story they tell. Gallant is bold and brave, with a strong sense of duty—qualities I admire.

I would be grateful if you could post your comments and review on Amazon. Any feedback you provide on the characters in the series would be helpful.

Regards,

H. Peter Alesso

For notification of future books click the Follow button on the author page.

BOOK 7 IN THE HENRY GALLANT SAGA

Henry Gallant and the Great Ship

by H. Peter Alesso

The people of Earth are traveling to the stars to create a galactic empire, but two mighty alien species are poised to stop them.

The ancient Chameleon race and the genocidal Titans have found common ground. Their alien credo is . . . *All humans must die.*

The Chameleon are humanoid but have an AI chip implanted in their brain which gives them unique abilities. Henry Gallant's exceptional ability to interface with AI makes him the key to understanding their technology.

For Fans of *Gattaca* and Horatio Hornblower.

Printed in Dunstable, United Kingdom

65308233R00150